SAME
BLOOD

SAME BLOOD

❧ ❧ ❧

Mermer Blakeslee

HOUGHTON MIFFLIN COMPANY

Boston   1989

For information about permission to reproduce selections from
this book, write to Permissions, Houghton Mifflin Company,
2 Park Street, Boston, Massachusetts 02108.

Library of Congress Cataloging-in-Publication Data

Blakeslee, Mermer.
Same blood.
I. Title.
PS3552.L354S26   1989   813'.54   88-23193
ISBN 0-395-48601-7

Printed in the United States of America

J 10 9 8 7 6 5 4 3 2 1

The author is grateful for permission to quote lines from the following:

A *Book for the Hours of Prayer* by Rainer Maria Rilke, translated
by Robert Bly. Copyright for English translation © 1981 by Robert
Bly. Reprinted by permission of Harper & Row, Publishers, Inc.

"Play It All Night Long" by Warren Zevon. © 1980 Zevon Music
(BMI). All rights reserved. Used by permission.

This is a work of fiction, and all of the characters in this book
are fictional.

For my mother and father

for their unfailing, specific support

and for Hansen

for his unabashed assertion of his presence

You love most all those who need you
as they need a crowbar or a hoe.

> —from *A Book for the Hours of*
> *Prayer* by Rainer Maria Rilke
> (translated by Robert Bly)

There ain't much to country livin' —
Sweat, piss, jizz, and blood.

> —Warren Zevon

Special thanks to

Dick Humphreys; my family, Carol, Jeanne, Kathleen, Bob; my clan, Joseph, Eeo, Thomas, Ani, Annette; T.G.; Jean Naggar; my editor, Signe Warner Watson; my teachers, Maharishi, Popsy, Richard Enemark, Peter Nelson, Robert Bly, Sallie Caldwell, co-workers in D.H.'s workshop; Gurumayi; and, of course, Eric.

Contents

xii

PART THREE

PART ONE

1

To Daddy

I'VE JUST ABOUT always cleaned houses for a livin'. Now I
clean Mrs. Butler's full time. I git $5 an hour and Mrs. Butler
complains all the time. She says things like, "It was three after
when you came in, dear. I hope you take that into con-
sideration." On Fridays, she don't talk to me till after she's
paid. Then she'll go on 'bout what needs to be done the next
week. How she puts it, she won't pay for talkin'. But I pay for
listenin'. That's how it is. I gotta clean. I ain't got a husband
and I got a kid, Bubby. He's three. And he wants me more'n
I got to give him. But we live in a good place, right on Main
Street in Hazel over the hardware store. We got three big
rooms, one been made into a kitchen. It's good for Bubby
'cause he can't hurt nothin'—the floor, it's linoleum.

I don't clean much after I come home. I said to Adele—
she come in after we went down to Joey's for pizza—I says
to her, "I git all my cleanin' urges outa me by the time I git
home, so I ain't tempted here to succumb." 'Cause succumb
it is when I git goin' at Mrs. Butler's. I take her on. I turn

fanatic, cleanin' what's already clean. My place, you can't git clean, it ain't the type. It's been old too long, you vacuum the windowsill and the paint, it come off in strips. The linoleum is the old kind in squares and most of 'em is raised up on the edge, which Bubby likes 'cause he runs his race cars along 'em like they're streets with square turns like in Cartsdale, where the policeman got us for Bubby not settin' in a car seat. Bubby took out his gun and shouted, "Stick 'em up!" and ever since, that policeman, he's been in one of Bubby's cars. So anyway, my floor's dirty, with that kind of linoleum nothin' you can do. But it don't matter, my rooms are big and we got lots of windows and the ones that ain't picture windows I open wide and I set down on the blue denim couch in my kitchen and listen to the trucks go by.

Sometimes while I'm settin' there, Bubby'll say, "You be Bubby, I be Daddy," and then he talks real low. "I'm goin' to work," he says and gits his red jacket on and he gits on his horse, though he's gotta keep one foot down 'cause the springs is broken, and he says, "Cry!" and I cry. He tells me everything to say and then I call him Hitler and he says, "I not Hitler, I Daddy." We do sump'n like this every night and then I git up to cook dinner, but I have to stand on the rubber rug I put on the floor under the stove and sink. That's the boat and the whole kitchen floor's water and when I go to the refrigerator my feet git wet and then Bubby, he takes off my shoes and socks and that's how I keep him off the counter so I can work free.

Sometimes I git him a cucumber at the Victory which he loves more'n anything 'cept chips and then no matter what we're playin' he gits the chair to stand on, gits his sword from the drawer which is just a small knife with a white and gold handle and he cuts the "cumber," he calls it, into slices and I gotta try then to like my slices thick.

I feel stupid goin' on like this but this is my life and Marilyn, she's the lady from Social Services who comes to talk and to make sure I don't have no more kids, she told me I should git out what I feel or she says I'll take it out on Bubby. Now I never hit Bubby 'less he's bad, and I told her that. Like last night, he takes the potatoes off the counter and throws 'em out the window when he knows damn well I'm just about to peel 'em. I always give him a warnin' though. I didn't whop his behind till the third potato went flyin'. And I know when I'm hittin' him he's just askin' for it so I'll stop cookin' and start in on him. So I said to Bubby, I says, "Why you wanna git me mad?" But he keeps on screamin' and then I hold him and we go downstairs and git the potatoes off the pavement and we got a lot more to peel then. We do it together though it's a pain in the neck, he wants my sword, seein' how well it works. I say, "It ain't the sword, Bubby," but he don't see it.

Marilyn, she comes here 'cause I been into trouble. Even how Bubby come I knew was wrong. It was Scooter Hall, and his wife is hangin' on nothin'. He don't care, he rides around in his red pickup drinkin' beer breakfast lunch and dinner, and yells at all the young girls gittin' outa school. He's there every day quarter of three. But he come home with me one night after he followed me to the Victory and I was wearin' a tight pair of jeans and he was whistlin' to me outa his truck and I give him the eye 'cause I'll be straight, I like it when a man looks. And Scooter, he's got that long hair and beard and a body like a sixteen-year-old with them narrow hips and not a hint of belly, how he saunters and sasses. I felt real sexy, him sayin' stuff to me 'bout how I'd move under them jeans. I didn't care nothin' 'bout them stories, and his three kids and his wife settin' home with nothin' but a TV. Them thoughts flew clear outa my head like a potato out the window and just like with Bubby there's someone backa me sayin', "Don't you keep on," but sump'n even stronger is drivin' me to it. So I give him the eye so he knowed to follow me home in his truck.

He brings in a six-pack of Genesee and we drink it on the couch with me settin' on his lap feelin' real good with all that hair. Now Scooter's a man would have to live deep in the woods to stay from trouble. He's got them bright, crooked eyes. I say, "Scooter, you the same as you was in eighth grade, you was wild then, stealin' stop signs off Clay Hill, people coulda died." He don't say nothin', just unzips his pants and pulls mine down past my knees and swings on top of me and gits both his hands under my bra though it wasn't undone so it hurts some but I'm just so glad he's gonna do it I don't care how I feel. I was dry as a bone when he stuck it in and I remembered Omar gittin' stuck in Ginger, our dog, 'cause I tried to kick him off her, and Omar, he fell sideways so they was butt to butt, Omar howlin' away sump'n wicked 'cause it musta been twisted in there, and Ginger, she started runnin', draggin' him behind, his butt to hers. It took over an hour 'fore Omar fell out, all the time him howlin' and she runnin' through the pasture and under the tractor.

So Scooter's humpin' away and I ain't gittin' any wetter but it don't matter 'cause it was over soon and he come down on me, his hands still squeezin' both my tits like they could pump milk. He was passed out and I felt almost lucky, like you'd feel if you saw an animal, a woodchuck or sump'n, asleep under a tree, like you was peerin' in on sump'n supposed to be reserved for God, but not the church God dealin' out love and justice but the God who ain't proud, the God who's like grass, who don't care 'bout people tramplin' over him or gittin' cut down, don't give a hoot 'bout growin'.

I tried to tell myself it ain't true, but I knew. I started gittin' big and I tried to hide it till it was too big. I set off to work for Tappen 'cause he's all the way out to Sweet Hollow, a mile straight up on Close Crick Road—that's where the crick starts in a little brook. It was Adele, she's always kept an eye out for me, it was her told me Tappen needed a worker. He's always

needin' a worker when it's warm, he's got a greenhouse business and a couple acres of corn, potatoes, you name it, he's
got a few milk cows left, too. I remembered we used to play
there every summer when we was kids, seemed everbody played
there, though it wasn't a nursery or nothin'. Tappen give me
work in the back doin' just 'bout anything from haulin' boxes
to diggin' dirt. I didn't work with no customers—I don't know
names or nothin' much 'bout flowers—and no one barely saw
me 'cept at the store but I wore Beulah's—Tappen's wife—
I wore her coat and she's mighty big. Beulah, she seemed just
the same, how she'd give all us kids playin'—didn't matter
whose we was—she'd dole out the cookies, milk, sandwiches,
right out the back from her kitchen door, we was never hungry
there, boy.

When I started gittin' big, that's when I moved into the old
green trailer used to be Willie Craw's. It was pretty beat up
and I was payin' $150 a month but it was only six miles from
Tappen's so it wasn't nothin' to drive back and forth. Sharon,
she come over once, first time in a coon's age, and she takes
one look at my belly and she got so mad she left and never
called back. She said, "You ain't fit to be a sister of mine."

So I'm workin' back of the greenhouse one mornin' trans-
plantin' ivy geranium and I go into the john and there it is,
bloody stuff in my underpants thick as snot. I didn't have no
pains yet but I knew it was up and I drove home and didn't
tell no one I was leavin'. I had the kid. It took from that
afternoon all the way into the next mornin' late and I'll tell
you all in one word how I felt—scared.

Now I knew what Tappen had told me after I asked him
'bout mares stretchin' enough for a foal. He said you gotta rub
cookin' oil on the skin right around the hole. And that you
hold back the foal with both palms hard so he don't rip through
fast, and you watch for little white arrows shootin' out from
the hole. That's where there ain't no blood. Then you rub,

rub the blood in and she won't rip. You gotta be quick, he said. You gotta hold the foal back till the mare, she's good and stretched. So early on when I was still thinkin', I got myself a mirror and a stool Ma used to have around her kitchen and I took the green plastic off the table and put it on the floor by the bed, it just fit, and then I laid down and waited. The trailer seemed so narrow and dark. Beulah'd said to me — it was early on, I was six months maybe — she said, "Wait till you can't stop yourself from pushin', till you can't hold back no more."

That didn't come till mornin', after the water gushed out all over the blankets and I was so beat bein' up all night with the pains I said to myself right out loud, "No way can I push this baby out." I was gruntin' like a pig. I finally did push hard enough to feel it come down and it hurt so bad I stood right up off the stool but I squat right down again quick 'cause it was like a hard ball but big as a grapefruit right between my legs, stuck. I just stayed there squattin' and I counted like I used to count trucks when I was young sleepin' on the porch. Then when I saw my lips swell up big, I knew it was close and I put my hand down there and tried to push against the head but it felt like my skin was on fire and I wanted him out, I couldn't stop to rub or think to rub, I just 'bout caught him he was so slippery. But there was only small tears, I guessed later, 'cause I stopped bleedin' pretty quick.

He was blue and I started suckin' out the gunk from his mouth and nose. I didn't even think to myself, *Gee, it's a boy!* I just kept spittin' the gunk onto the plastic which I can still see like it was yesterday 'cause I remember thinkin' as I spit how the plastic was all bunched up, olive green, and the blood and mucus swirled so it looked like Elvis Presley's shirt in the picture Sharon used to have up in her room made of that crushed velvet. Sharon said that the shirt design was his face but it looked to me with them wrinkles in it like a sunrise or

sump'n in space you can't see but would be just spectacular
if you could. Those three or four minutes I didn't know if he
was gonna breathe right, they was like slow motion, like I was
surrounded in water, everything suspended like, and me thinkin'
dumb thoughts. I didn't do nothin', just laid there with my
baby 'gainst me half sleepin', never would nurse steady. It ain't
easy holdin' a tit put in his mouth so it won't fall out or smother
him.

He was so little and I didn't know how to feel for him, I
had nothin' to call him, no name. I remember Sharon's kid
Jimmy, about two years old first time he say "hand" and gittin'
so excited he's sayin' it and holdin' up his hand each time like
it was a new hand now he knew the name. I felt all unfinished,
almost like I still didn't have a baby 'cause I didn't have a
name for him. But now I see I was so sunk in love with him,
I couldn't even feel it. Like you don't feel water till you move
your hand and splash or come out. He was still me then and
you don't go pokin' at yourself all full of mush.

Then outa the blue Beulah walks right through the door
into the bedroom still wearin' her kitchen apron. She had a
hunch, she said. I wanted to hug her and cry and have her
lay right there beside me but we ain't like that together so she
started cleanin' up the sheets till she sees the placenta layin'
there like a huge hunk of liver. I never even knew it come
out, the cord all white and blue goin' up to the baby. Beulah
went out huntin' for sump'n to cut it with and I didn't even
yell after her, tellin' her where to look. She was there now
and I felt it swallow me up what you go into when you collapse.

When I woke up all the sheets and plastic was up and Beulah
was there wipin' the blood and white stuff off the baby with
the pink washcloth I had swiped from her about a week before.
I felt like I'd slept days though it wasn't much. Beulah was
holdin' the little baby in her arms all wrapped up in a sheet
and she's sayin' over and over like one of them chants, "Bubby-

baby, Bubby-baby," and I think right then, *Bubby! His name'll be Bubby.* He just looked Bubby. I said it out loud and Beulah looked all red and startled like I had just caught her, fresh. She laid him down on the mattress pad beside me. He was sleepin' and I was starin' at him. It was like sump'n happened after the name come. All that love started movin', real slow at first but movin', like we was two now, and it built up so after a few days I wanted to eat him up whole.

II

So here I am goin' on and I don't even know who I'm talkin' to. It ain't Marilyn. And it ain't Billy, my brother, 'cause since he's been in Arizona sellin' used cars we ain't passed a word. And it ain't Sharon, my sister. We was never close anyway, not like me and Billy was, she's four years older'n me and she was always goin' off all dressed up, she'd look on me and Billy like we was animals compared, wrestlin' on the couch. Now she don't even talk to me no more on account of Bubby and since she married an electrician and they live in a nice Vemco home all carpeted and full of natural light, she thinks I'm as close to mold as a yam. Nope, it sure ain't her. And Ma, she's gone senile down at Mountain View which is more off than dead to me but I think now it's gotta be blood I'm talkin' to. It's comin' clear it's you, Daddy, 'cause we left off early. I was just ten when you got killed and I hadn't growed up yet and even 'fore that you never talked, you come home and head for that green chair of yours and we couldn't wake you up even after we got TV. You settin' there snoozin', seemed to Billy and me you was always hangin' somewhere over your body, like you never did fit into there in the first place. You couldn't've just died pinned tight under the dozer, no, it wouldn't've been right somehow. You'd have to go and be killed by an injection, a overdose of morphine they was gonna kill your pain with.

I can see me tryin' to say, "You'll be turnin' in yer grave, hearin' 'bout my life," but it ain't true, 'cause you dead or alive was always like Hide Mountain settin' there backa town. Even with the ski slope rippin' down through it, it looks wild to me 'cause of those caves off to the left where we saw a bear when I was eight years old. We was walkin' up to the slope 'cause you was seein' 'bout work for the winter and they said "too late" and you headed off into the woods, you was so mad. That's when we saw the bear and you looked square at him and said, "Margaret, there's yer first bear," and I was so much like you for that second I said to myself, "Yup. A bear."

Later, I felt more of that feelin' of bein' like you, big and full of caves like that mountain, and the bear was only one of the hundreds of animals — there was a whole bunch of 'em. You never changed from that. Even walkin' back out to where they bulldozed off all the trees for a ski trail, you didn't say nothin' though your face I remember looked almost scarred. It looked like that even in the coffin after Bunner puffed up your cheeks and pasted you over.

I remember Billy and me, we got the giggles both the same time lookin' at you layin' stiff in there and we snuck out the back of the funeral home so no one could see us, especially Ma, and we both had the same thing in our minds so we headed for the Tilford farm only a few houses down, both of us not sayin' a thing. We stepped over the manure real careful so our shoes wouldn't turn green and we'd be hit. Then we did that trick you taught us the summer before when we was all at Pete Teator's and Billy and me was watchin' the cows chew and lift their heads and stare with them dull eyes and chew and keep starin', and you come down between us and whisper, "Stare back and you'll go on through like jumpin' into pond water and comin' back up." And it happened. I was on the other side lookin' back at the three of us: we was real big, bigger'n life, and you was crouchin' in the middle holdin' us, standin' there like we was all the Poughkeepsie Bridge, your arms like them big steel cables and us the tall towers either side. It was all in a split second 'cause I surfaced quick and just as I come back into my own eyes, you said, real close to both of us, "You just seen like a cow but don't you tell no one," and I didn't.

But then every time I was upset, like when you and Ma was fightin', I'd go to Teator's either alone or sometimes Billy'd come and we'd stare and feel like you was with us again talkin' us in, and after, we'd feel all refreshed like we just had a bath. Problem was we'd git this weird taste in our mouths that was wicked bad, acid like, and I could always tell when Billy'd sneaked down alone 'cause he'd be spittin' the whole day. We couldn't help ourselves. Them eyes was like drink, like a curse. I quit when I was sixteen, fought like hell to quit. I knew it was bad, would do me in.

Beulah and Tappen's been good to me, Daddy. After Bubby was born, I stayed right in their house and it seemed all natural like Beulah was my ma. She got down a box of diapers from the attic. She don't throw nothin' away. She taught me how to put the pins in right, I'd never done it before and I felt all new and not brave at all like when I felt like you.

After a week there though, Tappen walks into the room we was stayin' in and says, "You gotta go to a doctor, you gotta go to the town clerk and you gotta git a birth certificate." Now Bubby, he looked pretty fat and the yellow in his skin'd gone, he was almost pink, but I knew Tappen was right. I knew there was sump'n if I didn't do Bubby would die even if he looked and felt to me OK, I couldn't really tell — they knew all sorts of tests to do. Even if he didn't die now, he might later when he was full grown 'cause of sump'n I didn't do. Just as long as they didn't stick no needles in him like they did you. So I got into the truck with Tappen and went to the town clerk and that's when the trouble started.

Daddy, I ended up on a list of New York State as a child abuser for three offenses: failure to seek medical help for the baby (havin' it and stuff), failure to use that silver stuff in the baby's eyes in case I had VD, and I can't remember the third, actin' without a license, I think.

Social Services asked me who the daddy was and I wouldn't say it to the lady 'cause it was none of her business and 'cause Scooter's got three already and don't take care of them. He just ain't meant to be a daddy, never mind a husband. Now you probably thinkin' I'm just in love lettin' him git away but you remember Scooter, don't you? Even as a boy nothin' could tame him and he ain't changed, never will, like he was born whole, followin' his own rules. And he gits sweared at but let be, like he's as much a part of Hazel as the goddamn snow. But I suppose his wife don't look at him any special way 'cept as a low-down son-of-a-bitch. So this Social Service lady, she's gittin' so mad at me I couldn't look at her face no more so I looked up at the bulletin board behind her where two of her kids was pinned up and I started readin' the sayin's beside 'em: "Jesus Loves You" on a sticker and "God Helps Those Who Help Themselves" below that in the middle of a field of hay.

I was holdin' Bubby extra tight 'gainst my belly durin' all the questions and then I don't know why, maybe 'cause the lady give me the willies, I started starin' at him again sleepin' and his skin was so smooth 'gainst my shirt and 'gainst the metal made like wood on the lady's desk that he looked angelic, almost like he was dead he was so peaceful. I was starin' and I couldn't help it, it was like with them cows, I was switchin' over whether I wanted to or not, but not into his eyes, into sump'n real far down, almost like I was feelin' from his belly now and feedin' like he done to me.

Then it started, the grindin'. It come on slow, but it come on, like sandpaper in the gut, real soft, grindin' me down. But then it seem holdin' him tight 'gainst me, lettin' him suck made it ease up, go away.

The lady, I heard her say that I had to come back till they figured out my case. She was tryin' to smile and said, "Well, I guess it's dinnertime." See, I still had to hold my tit so as Bubby could suck, or it'd just fall out or squish up 'gainst his nose.

I ended up drivin' from Tappen's back and forth to Cartsdale in my big green Impala Tappen fixed up and kept filled with gas. It was almost thirty miles. My place woulda meant another six but it wasn't that made me stay with 'em. I just didn't wanna go home and things was real natural, better'n it ever was at you and Ma's. I only seen Beulah and Tappen fight once and that wasn't nothin'. Bubby, he fit right on my lap 'hind the steerin' wheel, nursin' most the way to Cartsdale.

Yup, things was OK till Social Services gits the idea I gotta git Bubby checked out for PKU down at the hospital. I was scared stiff, I tell you, them pokin' his heel. He was screamin' and my belly killed like a hole was bein' drilled right through. Then Bubby was supposed to git circumcised but when I saw them instruments lyin' there on the table I grabbed Bubby from the nurse startin' to lay him down and I run out the door with him under my coat and Social Services calls up Tappen that night and I had to go back down to Cartsdale to be ed-ucated. I did every Tuesday and Thursday, but Bubby, he never did git cut. Daddy, you mad? I guess you musta been cut. They said everybody was and Bubby'd be called weird.

'Bout two or three weeks later, I left Tappen's for my trailer, I hadn't worked since Bubby come. Then they started visitin' me, a whole string of people from Social Services. Even after I moved again, outa the trailer to this place smack in the middle of Hazel. I finally told one of 'em who the daddy was, otherwise they'd cut off my support 'cause I didn't have "good cause." Then after two years of new people every month, I git Marilyn. She's come eight and a half months now, first twice a week but now twice a month. You see, it don't look good when you got three counts of abuse 'gainst you. Marilyn come in and ask all sorts of questions just like the others and I'd answer but I never did tell her 'bout the bellyache, how it would come on strong anytime Bubby was away from me, even if Beulah had him, or whenever he got hurt, like when he cut his cheek open on the kitchen closet, I thought my gut was gonna wear right through, or even if I was hittin' him when he was bad, my belly'd start up and he'd just lay there on the floor sweatin' like a hog.

Marilyn though, she ain't bad, she's the first one would sit down and act comfortable, like she wasn't sittin' on hay, and she's the first one would drink a cup of coffee. Maybe it's 'gainst the rules down there in Cartsdale. She asks Bubby things, too, what he likes. He thought about it first time, was quiet, then blurts out like he does everything, "I like trees, mommies, girls." Marilyn liked that, it seemed, and that's all you gotta do for Bubby, he's such a pleaser. He goes and shows off for her with a whole list of stuff—garage, barn, birds, house, truck, —thinkin' he's still real cute sayin' everything he can name.

It was Marilyn got me the job cleanin' for Mrs. Butler. She said it was important 'cause I refused to put needles into Bubby so he ain't got his vaccinations, and after so long tryin' to change my mind, Marilyn said I'll lose my Medicaid and maybe even my cash grant. Then I ain't got nothin' and already bein' on probation as a child abuser they could take Bubby away since I ain't capable of keepin' him, how Marilyn put it. Now they just see me as stubborn ornery, but I'll never forget, Daddy, how one minute you was there and the next you was frozen stiff as a board. I do my best to listen to the doctor and I let him check Bubby over but I stop short at lettin' needles go in. But so no one can say I ain't capable of keepin' my own son, I git this job. I was in debt anyway up to my ears, with rent here in Hazel $200 and the cash grant $305, even though we been lucky, Adele givin' us beds. Well, just the Impala — I got it from Oby Shader over in Kaatersville — it's in the shop more'n not. So I call up Adele, Beulah had told me 'bout how she was takin' in kids, her six were grown and she needed the money bein' all by herself and she's always loved kids. Adele, she said she'd take Bubby on for $10 a day. Adele's the one told me 'bout Mrs. Butler bein' so fussy.

Now Marilyn fought for me, got me up to $5 an hour, a lot more'n Tappen could ever pay, so I make out good money-wise but it ain't never been good on Bubby 'cause he cried like an Indian for three weeks and the grindin' in my belly got so bad I was near to faintin', and you know I ain't the type to swoon. Adele, she said, "Bubby's got spirit, we know that, he don't give up." Now she's seen a lot of kids, Daddy, and she said that Bubby ain't like others. He ain't like a kid, he's like a man. Sweats like a man, too. Why he goes through two, three shirts a day. Me, I don't know no other kids. You know I never took to 'em, couldn't stand babysittin' like Sharon done for money.

Them three weeks Bubby cried I knowed by my belly I was breakin' him, the little Bubby layin' there half an hour old that run under my feelin's like a bed of rock. Every day I knowed it was bein' chipped away, the muscle holdin' us together gut to gut like them steel cables on the Poughkeepsie Bridge. We was breakin' and I didn't like it. My tits hurt so by five o'clock, I could barely talk or stand straight and it wouldn't let up till Bubby'd sucked over an hour. They wouldn't dry up like decent tits woulda. Marilyn, she said they would. That we'd both git used to the new schedule. But every day they'd bulge up outa my bra hard and I'd go into Mrs. Butler's bathroom and squeeze the milk into the sink though I had to lean way in 'cause it sprays out everywhere.

It's goin' on August, five and a half months of workin' and

it ain't let up for me, the pains in my gut gotten so bad, I'm down to 102. Marilyn, she says it's better now 'cause Bubby ain't so attached. That it ain't healthy bein' so attached to the mother comin' on three. But I don't see it. Bubby don't trust me like he used to. He gits mad at nothin' at all, just touchin' his food, he blurts out, "I mad you," and points his finger at my head 'cause that's his gun. Sometimes I know he's just lookin' for fun and feels big sayin' it but most times he means it and screams and keeps it up no matter what faces I make, he says, "You bad, you bad."

I hate it, makes me feel I ain't doin' enough though I git so tired after work it don't matter what I feel. That's when I lay back on the couch and watch Bubby run his cars and trucks and talk to hisself. It ain't just the policeman he's got in them cars, it's a whole slew of people. He met Mrs. Butler 'cause I had to work extra for her on Sunday and couldn't git no one to take care of him, Adele was gone. So I told Bubby straight, "Yer comin' to work with me but stay close by or yer gonna sit in the car." Now Mrs. Butler's in one of them cars all the time along with Adele and me and his daddy who he don't know and Monga who's been with us over a year now though I don't got a clue who he is. All of a sudden you see Bubby walkin' with his head still as a dish and you know he's carryin' Monga on his shoulder. And I gotta keep an old broken chair at the table no one can set in, in case Bubby decides Monga's gonna eat. Anyway, I'd be layin' there and Bubby, he'd just up and quit, come over, and I'd lift up my shirt and bra and go half asleep while he'd nurse. Then he pulls my lids up and tells me short, "Don't sleep!" and I try not to but I'm shut down.

See, I nurse him so I can rest up. Otherwise I'd be havin' to play trucks and there ain't nothin' more tirin'. So Marilyn, she starts in tellin' me things and askin' and sometimes, Daddy, I git scared at what she's gittin' at. She says Bubby's gotta git his own bed, that it ain't good he sleeps with me, and I say that's dumb 'cause he wakes up like last night and he nurses even after my tits are outa milk and I go in and outa sleep. I tell Marilyn I can't see myself gittin' up and goin' to a separate bed, I'd be dead by mornin'. She don't like that answer, she says I gotta wean him soon or he'll be goin' to school nursin', and so I say to Bubby, "You wanna stop nursin'?" and he says, "No!" and starts cryin' and clingin' to my pant leg and I think, *Shit*.

And so I says to Marilyn, *she* can play trucks. I'd rather lay back on the couch and feel my body mauled over but my mind is sunk down in almost dark. But since Marilyn say it ain't healthy now, I don't feel good lettin' Bubby nurse in front of her 'cause he pulls the other tit up while he's suckin'. It can go nearly half a foot up and he laughs and stops suckin' to say loud, "TEE-PEE," then lets it fall again and the skin waddles awhile like a wave and Bubby says, "BOAT." He likes boats most. Marilyn, she used to wince though it never hurts me none, I got so much extra skin. So now we go into the bedroom where Marilyn can't see and Bubby's given my tits names. The left one, that's Bubby, and the right one's me and they always go places together, though sometimes they pull apart till I yell "OW!" and then Bubby stops the pullin' but not the game and one boob kisses the other.

III

Daddy, things've gone bad. Today you woulda been ashamed and proud of me all in one. I quit on Mrs. Butler. I didn't just clean for her, I done other stuff, too. Like today, I mowed her lawn, cleaned out the pachysandra, loaded up the rhododendron with cocoa mulch, whatever she says. She trained me from the ground up though she still watched, so even more than everything she likes done, I know how she likes it done, too. You gotta brush the ottomans off one direction first, then the other. Otherwise they'll be ruined, and the word "ruined" comes outa her mouth like all of England's stuffed in them stools.

Sometimes when I just come in, first off, Mrs. Butler's head looks real little settin' back against them big red flowers on the slipcover. And she's readin' her list and complainin'. Like yesterday, Mary Reilly hemmed Mrs. Butler's curtains up from the bottom and not the top like she's supposed to. Mrs. Butler was up all night. Now I do my best to think just like her to make me work better, so I could just about feel the shame in them curtains, but then goin' home I have to shake out like a dog does water 'fore I drive myself loony. And I see when Mrs. Butler's friends come, she switches. She's so polite then, you wanna dump compost right over her head, or do sump'n even more drastic that would make her heart stop, and she'd need you like she needed a doctor, or sump'n she couldn't pay for. Why with her friends she talks so nice, settin' there on her couch, she talks 'bout art works then or how the family ain't strong no more or how people don't die, they go on.

Anyway, 'bout three o'clock she come into the bathroom while I got my boobs over the sink sprayin'. I do it quick now, three minutes maybe, and she lifts up her hand that got bent back like a garden claw when she got the shingles and ain't come straight since, and she rakes the air, sayin' "I am not going to pay for you to relieve your breasts in my sink" in that high-pitched wail of hers, like it was a sin. She wanted a whole day of free work outa me for the time I spent in the bathroom since I started. Now I never take no other breaks, and I always give way to her even when I'm mad like when she accused me of stealin' her pruners. Now how would I use a pair of pruners settin' over the hardware store on Main Street? But I didn't say a word back.

The worse was — I didn't tell you this yet — when I had to

bring her dog Corkie to the vet to be put to sleep 'cause he was fifteen years old and pissin' on the chairs. I had to hold him while Dr. Jensen stuck the needle in and I watched his eyes freeze over in less than a second and then I dug a hole for him where she wanted his grave in the corner by the picket fence and then I go pick some daisies and wild delphinium by the crick to throw in with him and she come out and says she ain't payin' for me to pick flowers. Now already since watchin' the needle and Corkie's eyes freeze I'm all tied in knots and all I wanna see is Bubby 'cause he can lift the weight right outa my body sayin' sump'n like, "Bye Corkie! Dirt on you now." He's like you, Daddy, he don't flinch. Me, I just hold it in till it come out like poison, or like Beulah said 'bout givin' birth, how you wait and wait and you don't push till you just can't hold back no more. Instead of Bubby though, she come out raisin' that same claw of hers and has the gall to make me stay extra for my time pickin' flowers and I say like an idiot, "OK."

Today it was just too much, Daddy. I couldn't stomach that withered old hunchback one more second, raisin' that hand like I was some sort of weed ready to spread in her house.

I walked out. I left behind a check of $97 but I didn't care. I felt like you again, Dad, walkin' down that mountain with all them trees ripped away after spottin' the bear and pointin' him out. I felt big and I was ready to take Bubby huntin' if that's how I had to feed him. I remember you and Willie Craw talkin' how gray squirrel tastes just like chicken. So I pick up Bubby all cocky 'cause I'm free and it's summer and warm and I'm tellin' him how we can go live in a tent backa Tappen's—in the black-eyed Susan field, he won't mind—and no one's gonna disturb us. I'll git a gun and maybe even Scooter would come and teach us how to shoot. Course I ain't thinkin' 'bout September and October nearin' and how this big old Impala we're settin' in is gonna break any minute and

I still ain't paid Don Cramer for the work he done on it in June. We git home all punchy and there's Marilyn waitin' on the stairs more dressed'n usual in one of them shiny beige blouses.

Daddy, she tells me straight out I'm in trouble. That I gotta go git a shot of hormones to dry up my tits or they'll take Bubby on account of sexual perversion. I couldn't move. All that big feelin' drained outa me quick as a vacuum had done it. I threw up, Dad, right on the ground in front of them stairs. In front of that shiny blouse. And she stands up and holds me like I'd fall down without her and then she goes on 'bout how the appointment is already set with Dr. Muller down in Clem Cove and that I'll be much happier after it's all cleared up, like it was a disease. I felt so beaten down and ugly in the face of my vomit and Bubby glued to the railin', the sweat on his gut growin' his shirt dark. He knowed his ma ain't ever gonna carry her own gun. Then, like someone else is sayin' it, I say, "OK," and Marilyn, she gits in her little blue car and backs out the driveway on her way home to Cartsdale. I didn't even swear at her. I didn't say a word. I said OK.

Now Bubby's asleep, Daddy, and you git the whole mess right on your lap. It's all one word again — scared. I feel scared.

I bet you never knew when you was alive I could talk so, but with you it's just like with Bubby — I don't have to talk 'cause we're blood, same blood, and all the words are gonna git to you whether I talk 'em or not. But I ramble on to Bubby, too, 'cause it's same as that love I told you come when Bubby was born — talkin's like splashin' water with your hand, makes it feel even more waterish. Oops, Bubby's wakin' up, Daddy. I gotta nurse him. I don't want him to git cryin' how he does when he can't find me and it's dark. And it's our last night.

It's been almost a whole day since the needle come. My breasts swelled up hard and died down like a set of lungs movin' slow.

Then I laid back on the black vinyl and I seen it, Daddy, the bear. He got shot by one of them city hunters you hated. Wouldn't stalk him like a decent man into the woods, wouldn't travel his land. He tricked him instead with that bear lure you said ain't no part of a true hunter's pack. Daddy, Bubby's dead. They found a hole in his belly after he fell smack on his face on Adele's floor. Stone cold and white. Adele, she rushed him down to Cartsdale and they called me at Dr. Muller's. They say it's a hole been wearin' through a long time but I know it was the needle finally done it—same day, Daddy, same time. They couldn't figure out why he didn't hurt, why he didn't complain. I tried to tell him, the doctor, I told him 'bout Teator's cows and how you'd taught us to switch over and what we seen then. I told him 'bout the Poughkeepsie Bridge and them steel cables holdin' us together. I told him it was me the whole time feelin' the pain, I had switched over—it was by mistake, I couldn't help it—it was me felt his belly grindin' down, it had worn through, when the needle come. It was the needle ripped it, ripped me right outa him, ripped us apart, the needle. Adele come and hold me and set me down and I had to wait on the bench outside the operatin' room. Like I was at a dentist, a magazine layin' there on the stand next to me and the lady's teeth on the cover was so white, Daddy, and big, like they was gonna eat me up.

Then one of them nurses come out and says, "He's gone," and, "I'm sorry," and I ain't thinkin' nothin', I follow her in and see a sheet stretched over a lump—coulda been a pillow. They couldn't even leave him for me, Daddy. Soon as he left, they go and put a sheet over him and I had to lift it to see him. But he was gone. My brain didn't feel nothin'. Like the bone in my forehead right over my eyes got real big and hard. Or like I missed a sentence in one of them word problems at school and I couldn't finish, go on.

I was tellin' Adele—she was drivin' me—'bout watchin'

Bubby and switchin' over and 'bout when I switched first time with you and Billy, how for a whole second I saw us all three standin' there strung together but lots bigger, and then how I come up again into my own eyes, and Adele brings me to my house and tucks me in bed like I'm loony but I know I ain't. Now it's near dawn and I keep hearin' Beulah singsongin', "Bubby-baby, Bubby-baby." I gotta go, Daddy. I can't talk no more. Bubby's gonna wake up on the other side like he's surfacin', comin' outa pond water. I can feel him savin' up to blurt out a "bye!" and I gotta be ready to hear him 'cause I know without a body, he's gonna turn his muscle loose on me, yank me up outa bed and into the kitchen and yell at me for gittin' my feet wet 'cause the kitchen floor's water and he's gonna tell me step by step how to take off my shoes and socks myself and still keep cookin'.

2

Beulah

TAPPEN AND BEULAH'S PLACE is over in Sweet Hollow. You go straight up Close Crick Road a little over a mile, seems almost night gittin' up through now summer's here. The whole time the crick's gittin' smaller and smaller, till you can't hardly see it — what with the ferns and them yellow cone flowers grown up. It's only when you come out to Tappen's place at the top that it opens up again and seems so big, don't seem like a hollow no more. But then there it is settin' right there behind, Black Clove Mountain.

Beulah, she takes on kids like stray dogs. Had only one of her own, Laureen, and they tried twelve years 'fore she come. She don't ever visit, breaks Beulah's heart, too. "She was always mad when I'd take in a kid," Beulah said. "Never got used to it, seemed to git madder each time. And now, she never just come and talk or nothin', she don't feel comfortable." All the rest Beulah raised, seem they came to her outa nowhere, like me when I was knocked up. She just don't say no. Or like Eudora. Come there when she was ten, been there off and on ever since. Tappen, he goes along, he's always taken to kids though he don't push hisself on 'em. Four-H kids at Christmas, he's their first choice for Santa, it ain't just his belly, and that *is* sump'n to speak of.

I drive up and 'fore you git to the house or the barns or greenhouses, there's a big field shed open on the front, and there's Tappen, knee deep in I'd say a thousand boxes thrown under it he uses for customers to carry plants in. He ain't ever been the kind to stack. All 'round the shed and by every buildin' there's piles of those green plastic flower pots. Most is filled with just dirt but some got plants in 'em that don't look too good. Walkin' toward him, I notice most of them sad plants is chives.

"What happened to the chives?" I ask him.

"Them ain't sellin' like last year," he says. "Haven't seen you since the funeral."

"Been keepin' home. Beulah inside?"

"Yup. Brewin' up sump'n. You hungry?"

"Nope. Well, yeah. I came . . . Bubby, he . . . You got any potatoes?"

"Fer dinner or fer takin'?" Tappen turns to me first time since he looked up to see who it was comin' toward him. "We got bushels of red jackets."

"Don't know yet," I say. "Don't know."

Tappen throws his arm out toward the house, his nose back in a box. "Tell Beulah I'll be in."

Tappen, he's got an operation, I'll tell you. Four greenhouses, all with that double-layer plastic. And three barns, but that ain't countin' all the sheds he keeps God knows what in, he saves everything. The cow barn's full size though Tappen's down to only seven cows, been phasin' down, he says, for ten years now. The horse barn's in good shape, it's got a good roof, needs a paint job maybe. The farthest barn is the oldest, mostly he keeps junk in there, and some hay, that one don't matter much. Their house is a big three-story covered in that asphalt sidin', all light green. Beulah got panelin' put in the kitchen and livin' room. Looks just like wood, makes it real cozy, and they don't ever have to paint. The rest of the house got wallpaper been there since Tappen's pa and white wallpaper holdin' up the ceilin's, been water-stained pretty bad. But Beulah, she keeps it nice, plants everywhere stacked up on metal stands and bookshelves front of the windows. Tappen says every time a kid leaves, Beulah brings in ten more plants.

Beulah, she seen the car and she'd already gotten a box of sugar cookies outa the freezer. Like I was comin' home. See, Bubby hung around a long time, talkin', always talkin'. Three weeks. But this mornin' I woke up knowin' he was goin' off, and fast, like he was in a car all closed up and goin' 90 and I was on foot, wavin'.

"You makin' stew again?" I says to Beulah as I plop down on one of her kitchen chairs and listen to the air seep outa the vinyl under me and I feel good, like a lid's been lift up or is gonna be. Course, Beulah stays right at the stove facin' the stew pot and cuttin' onions. Seems she's always cuttin' onions, says they keep Tappen goin'.

"Thought you'd give up on us," Beulah says, scratchin' how she does on her left side. That's how people know it's her at the store 'fore she turns around.

"Nope," I says. "Just keepin' to myself. Been cookin' a lot. Then spend half the week eatin' leftovers."

"Want coffee?" Beulah asks, but she's already picked up the pot 'fore I can even say yup.

We was quiet there a minute and then I blurt out all at once, "Beulah, Bubby's gone. Just since this mornin'. I mean, really gone. Far. I got, seemed his last message: 'Git potatoes at Tappen's.' Sounded real important but all fuzzy. Long-distance, not like the others. I know it's the last thing I'm gonna hear from him."

"Margaret," Beulah says, sharp like, "Bubby's holdin' you up, ain't he? You been hangin' off his messages like they was a trapeze. What if he pulls you in?"

"He ain't gonna. He ain't like that. He's bossy all right, and he coulda hauled off and hit someone, but he wouldn't do nothin' 'gainst me underneath, just to be with him."

"Way you talk, he don't sound three no more."

"He ain't, he's dead."

Tappen come in and plopped down on a chair but no air come out 'cause the one he's settin' on got splits all over the seat and duck tape over that and more splits in the duck tape. Beulah, she starts settin' down tuna fish sandwiches front of both of us. How she whips the plates onto the table, like food come straight from *her*, outa *her*. I finished my sandwich 'fore Tappen even started in. He got his forearms leanin' 'gainst the table, starin' at his hands he ain't washed. Beulah fixed herself a plate and set down with us. She's stayin' more quiet'n I'm used to, starts wolfin' in the tuna. She don't have no tomato slice on hers. She musta give me the last one.

I ask her straight out right then, "Beulah, why you scratch so?" Thinkin' of all the time I been there, and I ain't never asked.

Beulah just sets there chewin', starin'. I wished I kept my trap shut. But then she pipes up, "It's the bull," she says. "The bull."

I looked to Tappen, who'd got seemed a quarter sandwich in his mouth he wasn't doin' nothin' with—he was lookin' down, lookin' at his red cap you can't hardly tell's red no more settin' there to his side. He wasn't gonna help me none.

Then Beulah says to him, "You tell her, Tappen. You seen it better'n me." She turned toward me, still chewin', and she says, "He was pitchin' up hay into the cow barn. It was, musta been thirty-four years now, after Laureen."

Tappen looks straight at me like he could see right through.

He says, "It was that time of month, he smelled the blood, knocked her down, opened her legs up wide, rammed his head right into her. Then he got her right here," he said, hittin' his chest. "He kept rollin' her 'round the barnyard there. When we got to her, Al and me, her heart was stopped, lungs collapsed. Doctors said it woulda killed most, but she stayed conscious through the whole thing, yup. Two pages of bones listed broken at the hospital. You ask her, rainy days she feels every bone."

"I know when weather's comin'," Beulah said. "Thirty-four years, we ain't never been caught surprised, not 'fore a frost, a storm, a cold snap, a heat spell, nothin'."

I git up from the table to git more coffee. "Never been near a bull," I say. Then I remember how Tappen used to call Bubby "little bull-calf."

"Tappen and Al killed him, of course, the next day," Beulah said, "but he didn't never go off. Come right to me first thing. Didn't even wait till I got home. Three or four nurses was there around me tryin' to lift me up, I don't know why, and then he come. Like he was pawin' at me, scratchin'. Right under my bosom, here. Tryin' to git in. Seep in however he can, little by little he was gonna git hisself in. I knowed it was him right off. And that I couldn't do nothin'."

How the coffee poured out of that spout, all bright and stainless steel, made me think of Bubby again, how when he seen I had a hole and the blood comin', he thought it was a mistake, God forgot. Scooter, too, pokin' fun. "Trouble with women," he'd say, "they got a goddamn hole."

"He been at me," Beulah said, "ever since. Been fillin' me up slow ever since."

"Never run from a bull," Tappen muttered. "They'll git ya then."

3

Doro

EUDORA COME HOME Friday from a farrier's clinic out near
Buffalo, but that ain't all she done 'cause she was gone near
a month. Beulah was in the kitchen smashin' shells to feed
the chickens 'cause their eggs is breakin'. Her arms was shakin'
like cake batter, her head goin', too, with the poundin'. It was
like Beulah smelled her or seen her outa the back of her head
'cause she wheeled around 'fore Eudora even made it to the
back stoop and the dogs started in. "Wouldn't ya know?" she
says. "Yup. My girl." Dust from the shells was followin' Beulah's hands around, surroundin' her hands like they was givin'
off smoke, white smoke.

"Beulah kidnap you again, Margaret?" Eudora says to me,
laughin' her big white teeth. She was born with teeth. Four
of 'em. Laughin' how Bubby laughed.

See, I never left from when I come over two weeks ago.
That's the way it is here, you come over for a afternoon visit,
not even supper, and you end up livin' here — they *got* five
bedrooms. I started work here again and gave up my place

over the hardware store. It was what is called a mutual decision, not an eviction, Dart said. Sounded just like talk outa Social Services.

Eudora's little, only five foot, and she ain't got a speck of fat on her and no breasts to speak of. I only seen her five or six times before 'cause she was gone off most the time I was workin' here or when I come with Bubby. I'll never forget the first time I met her back when I was here pregnant, I was walkin' to the vegetable garden and she was in the doorway to the horse barn. Standin' on the doorsill and starin', movin' up and down on her toes, stretchin' her calves. Like she was trouble, or a boy. She got boy's hair, real short, and though it looks brown indoors, it flames up red soon as it hits the sun. And her jaw, it's wide and the skin is tight over the bone as if she was 'bout to swallow or just did. When I come toward her, her smile got real big real quick, like a coffee cup just cracked under too much heat. We talked kids. "Didn't want any," she says to me. "So I said, that's it, and had my tubes tied." It come to me then what the Bible says, how people will one day say, "Blessed are the barren," and I said it right there and then, under my breath.

Seems soon as Eudora got here, things started up. Why Saturday, I'm in the front greenhouse 'bout to move a bunch of plants to the back porch and Eudora come through fast holdin' a wad of hair. Tappen's followin' right behind—he never run but he can sure step up his walk—and he's yellin', "Why the hell you want hair off Lucy's tail? Why it beat all." She's laughin' but don't say nothin', keeps right on walkin' out the back toward the horse barn. "Goddamn! I oughta charge," Tappen yells after her.

Only cookin' with Beulah that night did I find more out— well, I slice and peel, she's the one who cooks—and she starts talkin'. Eudora 'bout four times a year gits hair off one of the cows but this time Tappen caught her. He don't care much but she don't wanna explain nothin'. She goes up backa Black Clove Mountain with it. Stays all day and all night though no one can git it outa her what she does. Beulah says Doro — that's what she calls her — she says Doro's been readin' a book on this people way up top of mountains all over the world that didn't never die off, they stay hidden and don't ever come out. They pick one of their kids to teach what they know so it goes on. They can do all sorts of things, like see in on a table in a house two mountain ranges over, standin' with their eyes closed they know who's sittin' 'round it eatin'. They got sump'n goin' with animals, too. Beulah ain't exactly sure what but there's one of 'em can see, all a sudden, what a bobcat sees at night.

I was washin' my hands from the carrots that got too old and was all slimy and Beulah, she comes over, one hand still towelin' a pot already dry, and she says to me, she says, "Why I'd give my right arm to meet one of them people. Doro's had sump'n livin' in her room for years. That's where she gits her strength, such a tiny body and all. She says at night, right before she goes to sleep, it gits real bright and grows and grows, fills the whole room. And it wraps around her like. She gits real tingly inside and warm and she says she ain't small no more but fills out clear to the walls. Sometimes she says when she's real tired she ain't in the mood and she says just as she pulls the covers up, 'Don't you dare,' real sharp, just like that. And it don't. But then the next mornin', she sleeps late and she don't feel so good with the horses. I tell you I'd give my right arm to know someone who knew sump'n 'bout that stuff. And I ain't talkin' 'bout no books. And Lord, them North Hollow folk just talk about love and Jesus and the twelve apostles and I listen with these cows starin' me in the face with that look they give — you know what I mean — you don't know if they're settin' in your chest or if they're clear to the moon. But these people, they sound like they know sump'n, like they could be a cow themselves and everything else."

⚜

Reverend Dass, he been here 'cause Beulah's sick.

Wednesday, I seen it first. I come into the kitchen and Beulah's standin' there eatin' a peppermint patty, leanin' her hip up against the counter, her face just as pale. And she's got her garden apron on 'stead of her kitchen one. It was all white once but it's full of a brownish-yellow stain from her chest right down to her knees. It's got little red roses on it with tiny green leaves 'hind 'em. Hate seein' Beulah sick. Doro, she seen it, too, but different.

I was cleanin' Johnny's stall, scrapin' up the soggier stuff, and I feel someone 'hind me leanin' 'gainst the door. Doro just stands there, not comin' in, and I land the shovel into the wheelbarrow middle of the stall, and I'm just standin' there, too, starin' at her, keepin' hold of the handle. The wheelbarrow steamin' up white 'tween us.

"It's Beulah, Margaret," she says and waits. "Just like you hear Bubby, I see things. I've always seen Beulah real clear, clearest of anybody." She waits again.

"Keep goin'," I say, wigglin' the handle how I do on habit so the shit don't stick to the shovel. "Keep goin'."

"Beulah's whole middle, the left side, is all filled up with this yellow-gray stuff. I don't know what it is but I know it's no good."

"It's the bull," I says.

Doro nodded. She come in then, into the stall. She leaned back on the hay box made of wood, the top full of teeth marks and globber her horse Johnny carves out at night by cribbin', grabbin' the wood with his teeth and pullin' back onto his haunches, suckin' in the air with a groan-grunt could chill your brains.

"I saw it first a few weeks ago, when I first came back," she says. "But now it's spreadin'." Doro starts rubbin' her palms 'gainst them teeth marks, little half-moons.

"She's been in bed all day today," I says. "Only got up for the pot."

Good as dead, Beulah, I think, though I don't say it.

I see Doro's hands all the way pressed into them half-moons, just the perfect size for 'em, pressin' so her hands are turnin' blue.

"We gotta get it outa her, Margaret, all that gunk, or she isn't gonna make it," Doro says, her head shakin' back and forth, her eyes starin' off. "But I don't know, I don't know, don't know how to enter," she says, "how to get in to suck it out."

The wheelbarrow's smack in the middle 'tween us, still steamin' up some, and I ain't gittin' it, what she's sayin'. "We gotta get that stuff out, Margaret, or she isn't gonna make it."

There was only one last shovelful and I scooped it up and I grabbed the handles and rolled the wheelbarrow out into the walkway and it felt real good, felt good to move.

"You sleep on it," Doro says. "Maybe you'll hear somethin'."

"You headin' anywhere?" I ask, settin' down the wheelbarrow and cockin' my head back to her. I didn't wanna leave her.

She was starin' straight ahead now, in the stall, gone. How she faces everything straight on, face first, and always movin', hands movin', makin' it up as she goes. Me, I been backwards, been carried, thrown along my life backwards. I wanna turn around, head face first like her, but I don't know how, how to snap to.

She keeps rubbin' her palms 'gainst them holes in the hay box. How Johnny grabs on every night and pulls back, sucks in the air with his god-awful groan-grunt, almost sets right down on his hind end.

"Shit," I says and roll the barrow toward the back door, toward Black Clove Mountain settin' right there. This ain't nothin' I can fuzz out on. And I keep sayin' it all the way to the manure pile that's too close to the barn with the flies it pulls in.

"Shit, shit, shit."

4

The Healing

IT WAS CANCER, Dr. Brigham said. Beulah had cancer all through her intestines. He wouldn't hear about no bull. So Beulah said she ain't goin' back. And Tappen, he stood by her, though only after three days of tryin' to change her mind. But Beulah made it clear: no doctor, no hospital, no operation.

Every day I git Beulah outa bed and over to the chair. She is big, boy, and it ain't easy but after I freshen up the pillows and some days change the sheets, I help her to the commode we borrowed from Ida, Tappen's ma, so as she don't have to walk as far. Some days she wants to be dressed, too, and then I help git on her bra and underpants and her slip and her work dress. She can't do nothin'. Seein' Beulah with no strength don't seem real somehow. She went down so quick, only been a month since the first sign come, or since Doro seen it spread so.

After supper, Doro go out to finish the horses for the night and I go up to check Beulah, make sure she's still got a empty basin side of her bed. Then I gone into Doro's room first time.

It's real small, got just a single bed and a dresser and one of them closets come out from the wall, added in. She ain't ever had pictures in there even when she was young, Beulah said. By her bed is a little table, the wood all shiny, and a lamp with a red shade makes the room look almost cozy though it's hard to feel cozy 'round Eudora. On the table, there's a little book with a light blue cover called *Dear Heart's Sonnets*. Got a heart on the front with flowers all 'round it and a line of tiny birds flyin' through it look like a arrow. I picked it up. The back was all white, didn't have no writin' on it, just a black-and-white picture, a woman in a flowered dress standin' front of a fireplace. She looked real pretty, dreamy like, black hair all done up. Then I seen the name: Florence Benham Buell. It was Doro's ma wrote it, her ma. I set the book down quick. Doro come in. She walked over to the bed and set down beside me like she knowed I was gonna be there, like I was supposed to be there, waitin' for her.

She was lookin' straight ahead. "I need you to help me, Margaret," she said. "I'm not as strong as . . . as . . . you think." Beulah had been vomitin' up most her food and we both knowed if we was gonna do sump'n it would have to be soon, with how gray she was turnin'.

"I'll stand by you," I said, "but I don't got a clue what you're doin'." She turned her head, looked at me. "I ain't as smart as you think neither," I said. She looked straight off again, but she was smilin'.

It come out then, slow, real slow 'cause Doro ain't once talked 'bout her past 'fore she git here, never once. Florence Buell was the first mental patient at Burtrum General to ever git electric shock therapy, twenty-some years ago. And that was it, she never wrote nothin' after she was healed, how they called it, and she never saw nothin' again, like she'd done before, saw how Eudora saw, and she turned immaculate. Why, Doro said you'd kick off your shoes and she'd sweep 'em away and follow you 'round, takin' books off the kitchen counter soon as you'd set 'em down, it got impossible to make yourself a sandwich.

Doro hid more and more in her own room and that's I guess when it started. Florence — she don't say Ma — Florence started goin' into fits 'round her. Once she tried to cut the electric cord to Doro's record player with scissors so as she didn't have to listen to nothin' and then her dad started in, hittin' Doro for makin' her ma nervous. It was the worse on weekends 'cause I guess weekdays after school Doro'd be at the farm. That's where she learned to ride, even jump and stuff, and she'd go there every day after school and she could ride for an hour if she cleaned four of the stalls. She was the littlest one they ever made a arrangement for, and it started to mean everything to her to keep it, so that some days she'd stay late and clean five or six.

One day Doro went to the farm and all the horses was bein' loaded onto a big truck and the Petersons, they was who owned it, they was movin' to East Street in Cartsdale, into one of them ranch houses Doro hates.

All through that year she was ten it got worse and worse till wasn't a day go by Florence wouldn't break down and cry and then Doro's daddy would smack Doro across the face for startin' it. Florence called her "the little witch" and Doro said she started to believe it and then she started to like it so as one time she lost a tooth, her last baby tooth, and she saved it up in her mouth over an hour puttin' away the dishes 'cause she knew it was just a matter of time 'fore Florence exploded. Finally, Doro dropped a dish, a blue willow, and Florence, she done a first, she smacked Doro right across her face herself, didn't wait for Eudora's dad, and Doro, she spits the tooth up into her hand like it had just broke loose. Why, that set Florence hysterical and Doro couldn't help it, she broke into a smile, and her mother seen it, and that's when her mother broke down the final time so as her dad had to hold her down by the elbows right on the kitchen floor. Florence said the words then, on her back, her arms held glued to her side, she was havin' fits like she was bein' jolted right then by the current and she said the words "Her or me."

Doro stopped talkin'. Then out come a quick laugh 'fore she cock me a glance and gone on again. "Middle of the night before I left, I went into the flower bed and covered my face with dirt. Thought no one would recognize me." She was smilin' off into the room, almost seemed she could start rockin', but just her thumb was rubbin' back forth top of the other.

"I didn't really even know Beulah and Tappen. It was already dawn when I saw their sign at the bottom of Close Creek . . . I guess I thought . . . I'd been walkin' so long . . . See, they weren't the kind of people my folks would be friendly with. My dad, he sold natural gas and washers and dryers and stuff and they were talkin' once about puttin' in a pool. Except that Florence always bought her flowers here. She always had such a beautiful garden and she wouldn't buy from anyone except Beulah . . ."

Funny, it was just this mornin' Beulah was talkin' as I lifted her up so as I could see if she smeared any of her chocolate peppermints on the sheet. Beulah, she cracked a big smile and says, "Doro follow me to the kitchen that first day she knocked on our door. She was carryin' one of them little square vanity cases, and just as dirty. Such a funny sound come from her pocket, I said, 'What you got in there, girl?' Sounded too deep for change. And that little Doro goes and takes each quarter out, one by one, and sets 'em all down on the table real careful. She made eight stacks, eight dollars, she counted 'em over and over. Why, she wasn't even four feet high then, looked more like she was six or seven than ten. And then she says, kinda deep like, 'This'll pay for my food the first week. Then I'm mighty willin' to do chores for my keep, ma'am.' Straight outa one of them cowboys on TV. First time I done her clothes, I found a little piece of paper in one of her pockets, all wadded up and smooth as cloth, had them same words on it almost worn off." Beulah, she kept shakin' her head, sayin', "Yup, my little Dorrie."

"Come on," Doro said. "Let's go." We both got up from the bed and I followed her down the hall to Beulah's room real quiet even though Tappen was asleep on the couch downstairs. Seemed same as when I followed my brother Billy down the hall to Ma and Dad's room 'cause he heard the bed hit the wall boom boom boom.

We stood outside Beulah's door for a long time. She was belchin' 'bout every two minutes though she wasn't wakin' up, it didn't seem. We musta waited there near five minutes. Doro stuck her head forward, listenin'. She looked littler'n I'd ever seen her. Her eyes had gotten almost bright in the dark. We was at the edge.

Doro opened the door. A little night light was on, one Beulah always kept goin'. Beulah wasn't movin'. She lay there like a dead cow. She was so big and her face was squished into the pillow, looked like she had a whole bunch of extra skin.

I leaned into Doro's ear and said, "Didn't she used to call you Dorrie when you was a kid?"

"Yeah," she says, real low. "Yeah. Dorrie."

Doro took Beulah's hand from the sheet she had grabbed. The sheet looked all wet, wrinkled. Beulah was on her side and her other hand was tucked up under her cheek. Doro pulled it out like she was pullin' it from a wad of flesh, like it had been wedged in and it slipped out slow, like it was bein' born.

Doro held Beulah's hands in one hand and took mine with her other and I felt a hot liquid seep into my fingers. I closed my eyes and it burned and I breathed in and it burned and I breathed in some more and ooh it burned right up into my shoulder. I knew this was it, Doro had done it, she had made her way in and now we was gittin' it, we was gittin' it and I kept breathin' till Doro, she was on her knees on the floor, she was almost out and I grabbed her and I shook her loose from Beulah, I could barely do it, I had to pull their hands apart and Doro's hand was cold, it was stone cold, and she was pantin' and too weak to stand and I was holdin' her on the floor, we was both on the floor, we was on our sides, me holdin' her 'round the chest a long time like that.

5

Fever

THE FALL'S BEEN FUNNY this year. How the leaves turned. The bottom of Black Clove was still green and the top had already flamed up and blown off. So it was either red top and green bottom or gray top and red bottom, didn't turn all together like some years. And it wasn't even first of October 'fore most the color was gone. Maybe it's the healin' make everything seem changed. I know I ain't right. Though I didn't know it first off. I gone on two or three weeks just like it was nothin' come into me. It's only since Beulah's been out of bed seems I ain't right, more each day I ain't right.

Beulah seen it right off. She said to Tappen, in the kitchen first day she done the cookin' since she been sick, she says, "Don't you git at her, Tappen." 'Cause he wanted me to start up cannin' the tomatoes I wrapped up over a month ago, they'd gone almost rotten in the newspaper. Beulah, she started right in. Tappen had let a few of the green ones speckle up hard in the two frosts we'd had and she says to him that first day, she was almost back in form, she says, "I ain't picklin' no tomatoes if you don't git to 'em TO-night." Called gittin' to a man through his belly. And that night he done it, and Beulah was already startin' to pickle 'em, and there I am layin' on the couch, the ones been wrapped to ripen goin' bad.

"You let Margaret be," Beulah says. Then real low so as I can't hardly hear, bein' one room over, she says, "I seen her scratch. On that right hand. Why, it's almost raw."

"How you know it's the bull, Beulah? Probably a goddamn bug bite."

"I know him when I see him, Tappen, and I'm tellin' ya, he's got her. It ain't fair, him goin' to her. Wouldn't try Doro, no. Seein' Margaret all open, with Bubby bein' gone."

Tappen ain't sayin' nothin' though I hear him wheeze how he does this time of year, like he's breathin' through gravel, and it gits worse when sump'n comes up he don't like. The whole time Beulah was down he walked around makin' more noise'n a motor.

Doro, she come to me—I'd gone up to bed—she come in after she eat breakfast. She's just as fine. Come to tell me how to git rid of it, the gunk, like she'd know. So I says to her, "You don't know. You're different."

Doro ain't like Beulah and me. It's like she don't got a hole in her. Beulah says it's her tubes bein' tied so early on, 'fore she had any kids. But I think it's just her, Doro, the way she is. Beulah and me, we suck things in. Maybe why I got knocked up in just one shot. Even how Doro got married. Why, she told Larry "I guess so" when he ask her 'cause she's thinkin', "Well, this is next." And it didn't ever git to her. She done it like she brush her teeth. Down under, her real life gone on unruffled. And she the whole time seein' nothin' wrong, thinkin', "He's a good enough man and he lets me be." She knew he ain't ever gonna be rich, him bein' a sheriff, but she didn't care nothin' 'bout that, she was trainin' horses for money. Then he goes two years later, falls for a woman been raped that come into the station. And Doro says to him, she says, "Shit or get off the pot." Just like that and he left. Yup, blessed are the barren.

"Come with me up Black Clove," Doro says, and I says, "Nope," but I shot her a look over the covers. Her neck, it was just even with the doily on the dresser 'gainst the wall, like her head could just set there on it, on a white doily, and her body could float right out the door. "Nope," I says again. I didn't wanna go nowhere.

She clamp down on her face — what she picked up from Tappen when he gits mad — and she says, "All right, just sit there and don't do anything. But you listen here, there ain't no one can save you, so you just better pick yourself up." She says "ain't" when she wants me to hear.

I buried my head under the pillow. I says, "The bull got me. It ain't fair."

"That ain't no bull," she says. She stood up.

"You don't know," I says. "Ain't nothin' ever git you."

She walked out.

I stayed under the pillow waitin' for the dream to come. The dream that the healin' bring on, every time I sleep, same one. I'm swirlin' drunk. My little Bubby's there, short like he's still three but he's all dressed up in a suit and tie and holdin' a fancy pillow, look like a ring bearer at a weddin'. He's holdin' a little boy's hand — a kid almost the same age, maybe a bit older and real spooky lookin' 'cause the kid's skin is so white, dusty even, looks like he been floured. And every time you touch it, his skin, it flakes right off, like chalk dust come right off on your hand. Bubby, he's covered in it, the whole room is covered in it — even the air, filled up with that dust makes it look green. I was so drunk and I was followin' Bubby and this kid like it was Bubby knew the way . . .

I hear Reverend Dass downstairs. I knowed by her voice Beulah's sittin' in her chair, ain't gittin' up. He's blessin' Beulah like it been the Lord that save her. Beulah don't even offer him a cup of tea. She says, "It ain't the Lord, Reverend. It's my girls."

Beulah, she cries just thinkin' of it. She said to Doro after Doro come back from Black Clove, where she gone after the healin', Beulah says, "I knowed it was you. Then when I seen Margaret I seen it was her, too. How you done it, I don't know. Why you girls . . . you girls." She was shakin' her head. "You is sump'n else."

Doro, she said it was the name "Dorrie" got her in, what Beulah used to call her. That got her back to the first look 'tween 'em, that day Doro come and knock on her door. The very first look 'tween the two of 'em. She said it was that done it, she was in.

It don't burn. It itches.

So I says to Bubby, I says to him smack in the middle of the dream, I says, "Am I gonna die?"

He don't say nothin', just keeps walkin'.

I'm on the pot. There's a window looks right out to the barn, and then back of that, Black Clove Mountain.

I see Doro. Dumpin' the wheelbarrow into the manure pile. Sun on her hair turn it almost bright. Doro, a boy's boy.

It come to me clear then.

Beulah, even healed, she's about buried. Three feet down into this hole of a place, her kitchen, her plants. Like a goddamn rope's got her, by the belly. I can smell it, like you can smell nauseousness in your gut 'fore you vomit. Like I smelled Bubby in there when he first landed and I was all queasy. Doro don't know what it's like pregnant, how your belly turns swamp and starts pullin' you in and there ain't no place left dry to stand, loaded up so with that uncomfortable warm sump'n, real familiar. First as I got pregnant I knew I been there hundreds of times. And Beulah. She's like permanent pregnant. Been here swollen and bloated a thousand years eatin' bread and crackin' shells, like mud and rope's pullin' her in blind. Beulah, she'll never break out.

And then to think there's Doro. Standin' just as clean. Like a huge piece of glass you can see out of, see air, sun, sleet — hell, don't matter what.

Doro was shakin' me. Her forearms seemin' thick as a man's shakin' me, and her biceps, the skin so thin, see them rock muscles just as clear shakin' me.

I was on the floor.

I was bleedin'. Brown blood, what Bubby call hole blood. "Why, I ain't pregnant!" I say. And all that talk.

Doro's yellin'. "Get a goddamn pad on you!"

"Bubby ain't talkin'," I says. "It ain't fair. Gone when I need him. Like a goddamn man."

"Bubby ain't your man," she says, "and he's dead. You got to give him up. For chrissakes!

"GODDAMNIT! Look at me!" she's shoutin'.

"Why you screamin'?" I says to her. "Don't scream. I'm pregnant."

"For chrissakes."

"Like Beulah," I says. "Nope. Beulah ain't gonna make it. Buried, she's buried."

"Beulah's canning tomatoes," she says, flat. She's pullin' me up, steppin' me into the tub. The tub is so cold, ain't fair.

It's all dark! And my hands just as high, higher'n . . . My shirt, it's my shirt, comin' off over my head, floatin' right off into the air, *whooee.* "Daddy, too," I says. "He's gone, too. Just up and gone, Bubby and him, just . . . gone.

"You, you don't know, you're barren," I says. "You're a big huge picture window. Glass, you're glass."

"You been drinkin'?" she says to me but she knowed I'm right. Tub's fillin' up.

I'm holdin' my belly. It's gonna git soooo big.

Cold water. It ain't fair.

A red dot come out of my hole, float up near my hair.

It's real bright, bright red. Little round dot.

It ain't meltin'. My little round dot ain't meltin'. The water ain't clear no more. Water's turnin' brown, swamp water.

And my little red dot.

Yeah! I got it.

"Yippee!" I says. "Doro, look! In my palm. I got it! My little red sweetie."

Oh, poor Doro. Doro's cryin'.

"Yer washin' the window," I says. "The big glass window, cryin' like that."

She don't laugh. Old poop.

She's sayin', "No, Margaret, no, don't," over and over.

I see Beulah.

"Ain't a big enough bathroom for all of us," I says.

Beulah's got a plate of food. Scalloped potatoes. Wouldn't ya know? Yup, Bubby, potatoes. PO-TA-TOES. "Git potatoes at Tappen's," you said and that's what I'm doin', yup.

"Them for Bubby?" I says.

"Open yer mouth, girl." Beulah sticks the fork in.

HO-LY. Course, she puts in half a pound of oleo.

"Swal-low," she says.

"Swallow swallow swallow." Each time I say it a little more goes down, you can't help it.

"I'm pregnant," I say. "Just like you, Beulah." I hold up my little red dot. "See?"

It ain't there no more! I musta let it go! "Where'd it go?" I says. "Where'd it go? It ain't in the water. It ain't nowhere. I musta let it go. I musta killed it. I musta."

"More potatoes," Beulah says. "Swallow. Swallow."

"He got me, Beulah."

"Swallow."

"He got me."

"Swallow."

The cold water make me shiver.

Goddamn Doro, turn me into a cold fish.

Cold fish.

They were pullin' me up.

"I gotta keep lookin'," I says. "It's in the water. My blood. My little blood."

Beulah's wipin' me off, olive green, Beulah's colors. Wipin' off the swamp water, all brown.

"I'll dress her," Doro says. "Get her downstairs."

"I ain't goin' up no Black Clove Mountain. Meet yer spooks up there."

"You gotta wake up," Doro says.

"She still ain't swallowed all the potato. Make her swallow, Doro."

Doro was rubbin' my neck like she's gittin' down medicine on a kid.

Beulah's goin' on like a record, "Swallow swallow swallow."

The bird, I think.

bird

i ain't thinkin' i'm bein' carried

6

Black Clove Mountain

TAPPEN SAYS a little Red Rose tea and some TV. That'll do
it, git me out of the fever, how he puts it. Beulah just shakes
her head.

Doro says TV ain't doin' no good. That I could be glued
to the couch, for all the 'provement she seen.

Tappen says, "She can talk now, can't she?"

Doro says, "It isn't just talk that matters, Tappen."

Tappen shoots me a glance. "Well, it's a step, by God. You
got anything better?"

Doro walks out the back door. When she ain't happy she
goes outside, especially if it's cold. Stands on the back stoop,
her hands in her pockets and her shoulders hiked up, she rocks
heel toe heel toe.

Tappen don't follow. "It's a step, by God," he says.

I'm sunk in again but I ain't asleep and it ain't the dream that
come. It ain't Bubby. It's my own life. I'm fifteen. We was in
the butcher shop with Ma. We was talkin' to John the butcher,

my brother Billy and me. He asked us if we wanted to go into
the back and see the cows. They had just come in off the
truck. And we could see it happen. There was Lenny Hutt,
up on a ledge over a small standin' stall with two huge cow
eyes stickin' out from between the slats. He was holdin' a stun
gun, holdin' it straight down toward those two eyes. Snap!
The eyes dropped, and his foreleg, it drops, his hoof slides
sideways out under the bottom slat, he was on his knees,
and then seemed only seconds John's boys had him up, his
back legs chained, they was pulleyin' him up, hind end first,
and he was still alive, he was pullin' up his front foreleg real
slow, pullin' it in toward his chest, and just then Lenny
Hutt, he slits his throat and a huge . . . like a tub faucet of
blood pours out his throat and splatters onto the concrete
faster than it can go down the drain which is right below,
made just for that blood comin' from just that spot, and the
foreleg, it stops midair and then it all happens so quick, the
head comes off and the one guy I don't know the name of,
he slaps it upside down over two bars so the two clouded-up
eyes bulge 'gainst the metal and he digs in with a knife and
the tongue goes in one tub and the rest of the head gits chucked
on the floor 'gainst the wall and the other guy has the hide
near all the way off and while one guy takes a wheelbarrow
full of green and gray innards, steamin' up thick, off toward
a huge barrel at the front end of the room, Lenny, he gits
the chain saw and soon there's just two slabs of meat bein'
pulled along two tracks up toward the front near where the
shop is and the one guy is pointin' out to my brother how this
one has too much fat on him for his book 'cause how he's
shinin' under the long skinny lights and the other guy starts
hosin' everything down so as all the blood washes right into
the drain and the concrete is all white again 'fore Lenny gits
the stun gun pointed down toward the next set of eyes that
have watched the whole thing once already just like me, and

my brother rushes out the front and out past the refrigerated section with all the meat wrapped in cellophane and out onto the sidewalk, he didn't quite make it to the side of the shop where the dirt was, he threw up right on the slate. I watched him from behind the glass door that says Pull 'stead of Push to enter and I thought as I watched him, *I ain't like him, I'm cold.*

Then the rest come slow, come after Billy's finished vomitin' and he's standin' there with one hand up over his head 'gainst the brick side of the buildin' and I'm guessin' and I'm right, there's tears streamin' down his face, and I think real slowly now, like the thoughts are comin' through a thick dark paste: *I could kill a cow. Billy couldn't, but I could. Them eyes stickin' out, watchin' through the slats, seemed to shine so, deep brown, but they was already dead. Dead when they hit the truck.*

My dad hit my mom that night when Billy told him she'd let us go back there. He hit her in the bedroom so as none of us could see but we heard it. And we heard Ma, too. She wasn't cryin', nope, she never cried. She said, in the same cold voice I thought in when I watched Billy vomit, she said, "YOU and your damn cows. You gone and done it to them two, haven't you? Haven't you?"

He musta nodded or given her some sign 'cause we could hear her plop down on the bed like there was nothin' left to her, nothin' she could do and she let out a long dull ache of a sound.

That was the kind of night I'd curl down way low into my bed which was right side of Sharon's bed so as I could be alone with my hole. I went way in deep as far as my hand could go, and I shut out everything, everything 'cept me and my hole, my own tiny night, hidden there like some last place left over, forgotten to be filled in, like it was nothin' more than the drain in the kitchen sink, or like salt layin' out there on the table, everyday. But it was mine, mine only, and we was both hidden. Hidden and safe.

Doro, she stands smack front of the couch, her eyes straight on me. She wants me to git dressed, mittens and all. I says, "I ain't a kid, Doro."

She says, "We're goin' for a ride."

Tappen's pickup don't start till she fiddles under the dash. But yut, she got them wires hooked and she's got a shit-eatin' grin on her. She turns off the bottom of Close Crick Road up what we call Jesus People Road which is all frozen mud ruts so Doro's gotta go real slow past where the church is, then cross what was Rutkey's pasture and we're headin' for the loggin' road on Horseback, just left side of Black Clove.

I says, "You're gonna win this, ain't ya? You're gonna git me up on Black Clove, ain't ya?"

"This ain't no movie you're in, Margaret. This ain't no TV commercial."

"I don't like you sayin' 'ain't.' "

It's a loggin' road but it ain't used for loggin'. For five, ten years now, only ones travel it 'sides Doro is the Van Dusen boys, snowmobilin' up here any warm winter night the oldest boy George can steal a bottle of Jack Daniel's from The Old Caboose. The road goes windin' up till it hits what's called Devil's Ridge, a long flat ridge goes over a mile along the lower halves of both Horseback and Black Clove. And that ridge is why, when you look up from most places in the Sweet Hollow Valley, Black Clove don't look so high, not four thousand feet like it is, 'cause what you're lookin' at is really Devil's Ridge halfway up, ain't the peak at all. There's a spot 'long the loggin' road on the Horseback side 'bout thirty feet long where the trees got ripped away 'cause of a slide five years back when the hurricane Gloria come just as the snow was meltin', and you can look over onto Black Clove 'cause of how the two mountains're curved toward each other makin' like a bowl, and it looks real pretty, almost spectacular. This time, though, I look out and see Black Clove with no leaves fleshin' it out and it looks like only a skeleton of a mountain, not the whole thing. Seein' the rock jut out all over and every little dent naked under no leaves and every ridge and cliff, looks almost ugly, like a head without hair, how you don't usually see all the little hollows in someone's skull.

The only color left is from those pines, the ones lose their needles in the winter and turn bright yellow all through November. There's four or five patches of those pines along lower Black Clove under the ridge, but they don't seem to give off any pizzazz 'cause everything else is just black or gray or dull brown.

Once onto Black Clove the loggin' road turns up from Devil's Ridge only a few hundred yards through what's more a streambed than a road 'fore it ends in a pasture all growed up now with hardhack. We git out of the truck. We don't take fifty steps when Doro sets down. There's a little mossy spot under her but it ain't no place special, no place you'd pick to sit.

"Lost my virginity here," Doro says.

"No-o-o," I says and she starts laughin'.

I set down near her on a little rise 'tween two bushes. It's wet under me and it's cold, feelin' the wet soak in. Can't expect different this late in the year even though the ground's had four or five hours now to dry. She just sets there and I keep shiftin'. I ain't comfortable. Doro ain't movin', she just sets there, won't even talk.

So I talk to myself. I don't like this, I say. Not one bit, settin' up here in the brush, not even a view. Doro just settin'. I wanna git home. Ain't nothin' up here but a goddamn grouse got flushed out down below us, eerie almost, like a motor startin' up, or a drum, but deeper, almost scary. And

a chain saw way off. Probably one of the Choate boys, goin'
up onto the State land. It ain't I mind the woods, walkin'. It's
the settin' part I don't like. And she ain't movin' a muscle.
Lose her virginity, hell! Probably didn't even notice. Nope,
she's still a virgin really, down under, tight as a, as a . . .
Smells like winter. First as I smelled it this year. When the
ground closes up hard so it don't give off a smell no more
and all is left smellin' is the cold. Cold on grass, cold on
rock, cold on dirt. Cold! I'm gittin' wet, Doro, settin' so
long. Doro. Doro ain't here! Doro's gone! Well, that son-of-
a-bitch! Playin' tricks, thinkin' she can scare the gunk out,
she don't know, yeah, scare it out herself, she don't know
nothin'.

I scoot up a little so as I can lean back and not hit any
of the hardhack 'hind me and soon as I lean back, I feel
all heavy. Like all of a sudden I can sleep on stone. Like
my eyes won't open, and the air ain't air no more, it's solid
though I can still breathe, real slow, my chest movin' it, the
dark pushin' in on me, and my chest movin' it up down up
down.

I hear a noise. It's one of them cows comin' off the truck.
But no, it ain't, it's too young, like a cow weanin' his ma, a
cow can't come near its ma. Oh shit. It ain't a cow, it's a kid.
It's Bubby.

He's shakin' me, sayin', "Don't sleep! Don't sleep!" Pokin'
at my eyes, pullin' the lids up like his little fingers was tooth-
picks. I try hard but I feel like I been up all night.

"Wake up! Wake up!" He's screamin' at me, full of sweat.
Seems I'm hung over and don't wanna come to.

Then I seen he ain't dressed, naked as a newborn, and I
think, *Shit! I gotta git him dressed! I gotta find some clothes.*
I bolt up thinkin' he's probably peed on his pajamas and his
last pair of underpants. But he jumps back, seein' me set up
like that.

"You gotta say it, Ma. You gotta let me go."

I stare at him. I don't say nothin'. I know what he means, what he's gittin' at, he don't have to explain, I know. But I just set there like I got tar in my mouth. Then I shake my head no.

"You gotta say bye, Ma. 'Bye,' just like that. Say it, Ma, say it!" He's shakin' like a leaf, thinkin' I still don't know.

It ain't fair, me shakin' my head like I'm doin', not givin' a inch, makin' him do it all. I knowed it ain't fair, but then I do even worse. I lift my arms to him, I wanna hug him so and he looks at them arms and his face turns. First seems like he's gonna melt, melt right down into a six-month-old, right smack into my arms again and all mine, but then quick, his face, it goes stiff, his cheeks pull in and he's mad. Mad.

"No," he says. "You can't do . . ." and he turns his back on me. He's cryin'. Like he's almost broke, he says, "You ain't gonna let me go."

But then his voice, it goes cold, turns 'gainst me again. "And all this time I waited," he says slow, "so you wouldn't be alone. So you'd have someone. And you still won't budge." The word "budge" come out and I seen his disgust in it. And I seen also he wasn't three no more. And then I seen he was gone.

He gone and done it hisself. Took all his muscle to turn on me but he gone and done it.

Don't know if I'm more proud of him or more 'shamed of myself.

I scream out after him, "Yes. Bye. Yes, yes, bye. Go. Go on." But it's too late. The one last only thing I could do for my Bubby and it's too late. 'Cause I just set there shakin' my head. I just set there starin' at him, wantin' to just hold him one last time and then it was too late, too late to push him on, push him forward, away. The least I coulda done.

"Margaret, for chrissakes! What are you screamin' at?"

It was almost dark and I was full of sweat.

Doro was over me lookin' scared. "Come on, we're goin' home, Margaret, we're gonna go home. We can go home."

"We can eat supper," I says. "I can eat me a good hot supper."

7

Billy

EVEN THOUGH I ain't as crazy like when it was that time of month, Beulah says I still got the gunk in me on account of the healin'. It go right through Doro and into me. She says the bull's on to me, that he's got my scent now and anytime he gits a chance he's gonna fill me up, little by little. Like he done her. We're like mother-daughter, she says, just the way I am, I'm open, got a big hole, however you wanna put it, she says I'm stuck.

I know it myself, that he got hisself in there, and almost seem I don't mind. Maybe what Bubby meant, how I ain't alone no more, how he waited so as I didn't have to be alone. Beulah, too, she says, too, it ain't that bad. That it don't mean I'll git sick on it, cancer and all, like she done. And it don't mean I gotta go crazy again. Even with all the scratchin'. I knowed it was silly scratchin' my hand raw, 'cause the itchin', it was way in, too far in, all the way through me, like a bee inside a hay bale, no way to git at it.

"The bull's got you," Beulah says, "but you don't know yet

what he's gonna give you. It ain't always poison. I'm tellin'
you, don't you run. You'll be sorry if you run. I know."

She says I can't say no to no children. " 'Cause you never
know," she says. "You never know which one it'll be come
and set you free. Look at Doro, all she was was trouble growin'
up. Why, she got suspended three times outa Hazel and twice
outa Kaatersville till she drop out altogether and learn how to
shoe horses. And she was the one, she was the one lead it out
and you're the one it come to."

The whole time Beulah's talkin' children, she's thinkin' Billy
Hart. I knew 'cause I heard her on the phone with Shooey
Molton. A kid had been found. Named Billy Hart.

She don't say nothin' to me though 'bout the kid. Like she's
tryin' to be sneaky. But when Tappen comes in from takin' the
bush hog off his tractor and puttin' on the plow Beulah starts
up 'fore he even gits the grease off his hands and she's loud
enough for me to hear clear upstairs. "The mom was a Tilford
girl, married that Hart man from over near Clem Cove. He's
the one died of cancer last winter 'fore Christmas, and all the
stores had them coffee cans in 'em the Girl Scouts made to put
money in for presents and food for the family, remember?"

The water stops. Tappen must be grabbin' a paper towel,
he ain't allowed to use the tea towels with *his* hands. He don't
even let her finish, says, "Beulah, why you want another one?"

"Now Tappen, you listen here," Beulah says. "Billy's ma
crawled into a freezer and froze herself. Left Billy only three
years old locked up in the house with all the drapes pulled.
The dog finally broke out a screen in the back and the grandmother, Hart's mother, she come over and find poor Billy
almost dried up and all white. The TV was blarin' football
and the whole house was ripped apart. She done it, they say,
right before. Billy, he don't talk so they don't know what he
seen, or if he shut right down and don't 'member nothin'. He
was in there three days. Shooey, she called."

Tappen don't say nothin'. I could just see him leanin' back 'gainst the sink, pickin' the grease out of one set of fingernails with the other set. Beulah, she waits, openin' the oven door, shovin' must be chicken in, shuttin' it. Like it was all in rhythm, their own married rhythm — a burst, a wait, a question, boom boom boom. "Why don't the grandmother want him?" Tappen asks.

"She just don't take to kids. And she's goin' on seventy-eight. Her son was near fifty when he married the Tilford girl fresh out of high school. And Billy, he never did like the grandmother anyway, Shooey said."

Tappen kept dead silent and Beulah, she was shut up good, too. Neither of 'em knew I come down, was in the doorway listenin'. Tappen got one hand fisted up 'gainst his mouth and nose, his hands still look pretty black 'cause how the grease sticks in the calluses.

"Billy," he mutters. "B-i-l–l-y Hart." He catches sight of me lookin' square at him. "You got a brother named Billy, don't ya, Margaret?"

Beulah wheels around from the counter like she just been jumped on but then a smile come on her face.

"Yup," I say. "In Arizona."

"You want him?" Tappen says to me. "You wanna take Billy Hart?"

"Yup," I says flat, like I known it for years.

When I first seen Billy settin' on the livin' room carpet at his grandmother's where we picked him up, I closed my eyes. I didn't hear a word his grandma was sayin' to Beulah. I seen him and I says, "Yup." I seen first his black hair 'gainst that tan carpet. Then he looked up and I seen his white skin, and then his eyes that go in again real dark — look black, too, like pits. Black white black. It's 'cause his skin flakes so, makes him look even more white though they been feedin' him straight cream, cod liver oil, extra salad dressin', you name it, every kind of oil or fat around. Yup, Beulah, this is my boy. My boy Bubby bring me, leadin' him by the hand right to me. Yup, here he is, no fat on him even at three and a half. Just organ, bone, and little rocks for muscles.

Billy don't talk, not a word. Not even a "yeah." But boy, can he scream! He's the maddest kid I ever did see. Not like Bubby's mad. This mad is old, how he chomps down like he don't have teeth. And his eyes, they're sunk in, with the skin all 'round 'em yellow, makes him look even madder. Even Beulah's cats stay clear.

I clean out the boxes what used to be Bubby's. Give Billy one of his old trucks, ain't big and it's all beat up, but it was far and wide Bubby's favorite, his red truck. Billy turn, walk away, won't take it from my hand, won't even look at it. I left it right there on the floor. Then I seen he's got it in the livin' room which ain't a real room 'cause Tappen took out the wall 'tween that and where we eat, the kitchen don't have room for a table. Billy's almost hidden side of the couch, probably hopin' nobody'll catch him likin' it.

I'm gittin' out some potatoes from the bin to peel and boil up and Beulah starts talkin'. "He's choice of that truck, Margaret, won't let a soul even near it. You're makin' your way in, girl, don't you worry."

But I do. He ain't softened a bit. Like love ain't gonna make a dent here, not with this one. No matter the dream, no matter Bubby bring him.

Doro come down the stairs, you can always hear the steps clear as day from the kitchen. She's goin' into the livin' room right toward Billy. He starts screamin', don't want no one near.

She picks Billy up kickin', throws him under one arm, and heads out past the table to the back door, Billy's feet pointin' toward the horse barn, him poundin' his two little fists on her butt.

"Well, well," Beulah says. "There's a match."

That Eudora goes and gives Billy a little hatchet and she takes an ax from her tack room. And they tromp out, Billy behind, Breezie and Sam, Tappen's dogs, they was loose and followin', too, over the mud part of the pasture up toward where the hill part begins full of nothin' but woods. Doro doesn't even wait for Billy or look behind to see if he's cut off his legs, she just starts hackin' at the bottom of a poplar tree, or what Tappen calls quakin' aspen, just at the edge of the woods. How their leaves quake makes them trees seem they could only hold little tiny birds, even with their trunks, little chickadees, or sparrows, how those stems hang them leaves. And she's hackin' away for no good reason I can see and Billy's caught up now just starin' at her. I catch up from behind, too, and Billy and me just stand there watchin' her, not sayin' nothin', and she cuts the whole damn tree down and just as it falls, wouldn't you know, Billy gits this huge grin 'cross his face like I ain't seen a hint of since he come. All the leaves flop down toward the ground so only their backsides show not even a pale green in the sun but white.

Doro hands me the ax like it was all natural what she done and like it was my turn and I took it, like I wasn't thinkin' nothin' funny neither. Like I was doin' sump'n practical. Not only that but I says, right out loud, "Come on, Billy," and I start hackin' at the limbs almost fierce and Billy starts on the smaller branches and every part of me forgets he's still a month short of four.

We strip that thing into a long hefty pole and two piles of branches and twigs.

"That's YOUR ax, Billy," Doro says. Then she adds, quieter, "But don't you let Beulah see it."

All the way back to the barn, he got his elbow cocked up toward the sky so as the blade don't once hit the ground.

*

Sleepin', Billy's face changes. I lay down there with him and I watch the line he ain't supposed to have, bein' just a kid, pointin' up into his forehead, deep. I watch sleep fill it in front of me, like wind fillin' in a ditch, and he looks part child again. Little bull-calf.

His first words come then, sleepin'. He was callin' his Cheez Doodles. Called 'em under the sheet.

They was all over his bed when they found him. He wouldn't eat one of 'em though he was just 'bout starved, and he was real scared when they come into his room, hidin' 'em quick. Didn't want no one to see 'em.

Goddamn grandmother threw 'em out.

He had kept 'em all whole, wasn't one of 'em got crushed.

PART
TWO

8

Jo

IT COME TO ME finally I can't git along on $60 a week even if room and board are free for me and Billy, and even though I git just 'bout every bit of Billy's clothin' from Adele, who runs the rummage sale out of the Hazel church, she lets me comb the boxes 'fore she gives 'em over. Tappen, he ain't able to pay me no more, so he gits this idea that I could work for Ida, his ma, who lives a mile down bottom of Close Crick and who was lookin' for someone evenin's, and Beulah or him could watch Billy and that would be another $5 to $10 a night dependin' on how much she needed me, one or two hours. It don't mean I'm settin' pretty but it mean I can make it, and it mean I look OK if anyone give me trouble 'bout Billy.

Ida's ninety-two, used to be a teacher at our school. And she taught Sunday school, too, fifty-five years she taught that for recreation. Every night I do the same things for her, I git her meal out from the refrigerator and heat it up 'cause it come already made from Meals on Wheels. And I tear the foil on her Polident 'cause her hands've gotten so stiff she can't do it and then I help take off her clothes, her girdle and bra and 'specially the stockin's that keep her blood circlin' down into her feet so her ankles don't swell, she could never git 'em off, even I gotta really pull, and then I help her put on her nightie and stick her nitroglycerin square onto her chest and pull the old one off. Some days I gotta move the kerosene heater she got for the winter either closer or farther away and then I wash any dishes she might've used over the day and sometimes I vacuum just front of her chair and clean the toilet, though I ain't supposed to do any cleanin', and then I set down and do her feet. That's the important thing, she always says, that's what she's been waitin' for. I first soak 'em in a basin of hot water, then massage 'em with cream and spray 'em with Granulex she has to have a prescription for so as she don't git her ulcers back. Last year her feet were just covered, she said, taken 'em a whole year to heal, and the whole time she was needin' full-time help.

When I'm doin' her feet, Ida talks on and on even if the TV's goin' and that's how I first heard 'bout the other girl who come and help her. Jo, Jo Dailey. Ida leans down and though I'm the only one there, she says in almost a whisper, "Jo's what's called a caretaker in the town," and she sits back up and gives me a twinkle 'fore she goes on, "though her boyfriend, he don't pay."

Jo comes most mornin's without ever goin' to bed, does her little chores, and then scrubs Ida's back. Then she goes home, sleeps most the day. Jo and me, we're the only ones ever touch Ida since her ulcers been healed.

I'd seen Jo when I first come to Ida to talk over my pay and what she expected me to do. Jo was in Sharon's grade, Ida said, so she couldn't be more'n thirty-six. Jo didn't talk to me none then, just a hello, but her face, it was all laughy, cheeks swelled up and freckled, and squinty eyes. And her hair, it was dyed the blackest black. Even when she gone out on the stoop to hang up some of Ida's underpants, though they was gonna freeze, her hair still looked like it been sprayed solid. Jo puffs it up so it come out near a hand's spread all 'round her face, and where it hit her shoulder you could see her shirt, it was dark from sweat.

"All that sweat," Ida says to me. "Why, Jo is always sweatin', even now, November, perspires just pullin' up my stockin's." Course, they're the therapeutic ones, real thick and supposed to stretch but don't. Then Ida brings her shoulders forward, much as she can with her foot stuck out onto my hand, and she whispers, "I think it's drugs makes her sweat like that, that's what I think."

I'd been helpin' Ida near a month when one day I gone down early, wasn't even four o'clock though it was gittin' dark by five so we were eatin' supper earlier. There was nothin' Tappen wanted me to do and no customers come this late in the year so I thought I'd git Ida outa the way. I walk right in through the back, don't knock, and there was Jo, right in front of Ida's chair, hummin' away and whirlin' 'round on the green carpet with nothin' on top but a black lace brassiere, and Ida's gigglin', her hands up front of her face and her shoulders hunched forward and shakin' like she was the bad kid in the back of her own Sunday school eyein' dirty pictures. Jo, with must be a size 36D, was wavin' her arms and twirlin' to show every part of the black lace and a cleavage half up to her collarbone, her nipples pokin' through for the old crone.

"I bet you didn't know, Margaret," Jo says soon as she seen I come in. "Ida's only done it once." Her hands was swishin' over top her head and her hips was wigglin' away to her hummin', like she's Hawaiian.

I don't say nothin'. Jo's jeans ain't snapped shut but pinned with a big safety pin so they can fit 'round her beer belly. Don't seem they'd fall down or nothin', how they're pasted to her butt and hips which come out far enough to make even that belly look small.

"And she swears to God she was sleepin'," Jo says and then

she leans toward Ida and shouts kinda loud, "What'd ya do, honey, wake up with your legs spread?" Jo was laughin' so and I crack a smile, too, and Jo turns to me then and says lower, she says, "It's no wonder he took off."

"He was nothin' but a drunk," Ida says and sticks out her lower lip like she don't have her teeth in. She don't look mad though, she looks proud, proud she could still hear some, proud he took off.

"Ida's a fertile one here, Margaret," Jo keeps goin'. "Tappen come with just one shot." Jo's twirlin' for me now, too, facin' me. Them nipples seem 'bout to rip that black lace.

"Same like Bubby," I says, "just one shot."

Jo invited me over to her place when I got done at Ida's and on a whim and without sayin' nothin' I took my old green Impala all the way to the middle of Langdon.

Jo lives right on 209 next to the drugstore in one of the rooms Traver rents out. Ida used to live right over Chapmann's and that's how they come to make a arrangement. But then Ida moved out to be close to Tappen. Ain't like her son, she says, to ever git to town much, even Sundays. Jo, she stayed workin' for Ida, drivin' her car, an old Chevy Nova, right out to Sweet Hollow, which means some days she don't make it, and then Ida, she says as I come in, every time Jo don't come, she says, "I'm not too good today, no. Jo, she had one of her 'adventures' and I been so laid up . . ." And then she's off complainin' till I butt in and ask 'bout Jo's car and then Ida pipes up, "Why, it's a seventy-three," every time like I didn't know. "Starts only half the time, yup, just 'bout fifty-fifty."

Now Ida says she don't miss town, bein' that the trucks got so bad comin' through on 209 and with the traffic the ski slope brings in, but I think she misses keepin' track how she did, livin' right next to Jo, which of the boys Jo'd git to fix her car, she'd always find someone. Jo's got them black and white dice made of that velour stuff hangin' off her mirror. She's had them same dice in every car she's ever owned since she was seventeen. Jo says everything comes from luck, and it don't matter if it's bad or good, 'cause you can't tell which is which anyway.

Jo's got one big room with a kitchenette at one end. She's only got two tiny windows up high 'cause hers is in the basement, but Traver paneled the whole thing and she's got a real nice couch, cherry red and real modern, her mother give it to her. And she's got a TV.

Jo opens the refrigerator and just stares. "Miller OK?" she says. It ain't really a question but I still say "sure" as I take it from her. Then she says, "You wanna see what Vanna's gonna to come up with tonight? Does she dress to *kill*."

"Who's Vanna?" I say. I set down on the couch 'cause there ain't no other chairs.

"*Wheel of Fortune*? You've never seen *Wheel of Fortune*? And Vanna? Hell, you don't know what you're missin', Margaret."

She flicked on the TV. She set down on the floor cross-legged and I think her thighs are gonna burst right through her jeans and I'm almost right, she got little rolls started where the seam's gone weak. Pretty soon, since we caught it just at seven-thirty, the man come on and then Vanna, boy! How she keeps that smile goin' through all that arm wavin' I don't know. Even when she turns kinda, she still keeps smilin' straight at you, and just as she spreads her arm back the TV brings like a livin' room set right up close and then you can't see her no more, but it don't matter 'cause you're all glued in on what they got for prizes — not only furniture, they got matchin' carpets, too, or drapes, even a stereo or sump'n practical like a washer and dryer or kitchen stuff. They show a whole slew of things you git to pick from the money you make from the wheel spinnin' and comin' up with the right phrase durin' your turn. The phrase is always sump'n catchy, Jo says, sump'n you've heard, but still it don't look easy. You gotta guess a letter every time you spin — vowels, they cost extra — and then the one who guesses the catchy phrase after most the letters been filled in, they're the one spends all the money. Every time the wheel spins, Vanna, she claps and the audience is yellin' even though it might go to BANKRUPT or LOSE A TURN but mostly it's money it goes to and everyone yells till it stops.

Once someone wins, the showcase come up and they use up their money real fast like they're bein' timed through that part, too. And Vanna, she's back again smilin' — she never talk, Jo says — she's openin' this arm or that, or with some things she fades out altogether, and then next minute she's there again settin' on a couch, and wouldn't you know, her dress matched the whole set, everything was all rose-colored and her dress, too, but shiny and lots brighter.

"Ever got her layin' on a mattress?" I ask Jo, and she laughs and gits up for more beers even though I ain't quite finished.

Then they showed all kinds of kitchen stuff and at the end they throw in two shelves of cleanin' products so you can use up the last bit of your money and Vanna, she never lost that grin of hers and I says to Jo, I says, "Gee, I wonder if she'll git down on her hands and knees to show them off, too."

Jo starts laughin' and I says, "How she looks at the camera, why, she couldn't see where she was scrubbin'."

"Scrub straight through her gown," Jo puts in.

"Good time for a commercial," I says.

"Good time for a mattress," Jo says, and boy! We was howlin'.

Now Vanna's hair is beautiful, all thick and then it goes wavy at her shoulders, real blond. Jo says I should tease mine up but I says mine ain't like that, it's too thin to tease 'cause I pulled it out when I was a kid. I had two bald spots both sides of my head when I was in the fourth grade. I'd twirl it into a big knot so I'd have to pull it out and I got to like how it felt just as it finally broke and rip out, sometimes it'd be quite a wad. Ma, she'd find 'em on the floor by the couch or under my bed and she'd whop me one but it didn't do no good. So I says to Jo, "I ain't ever gonna have hair like that and I ain't ever gonna glue a smile on for a brand-new washer neither, or lookie here, an all-bronze rendition of a cat."

"Now I'd like that," Jo says.

"Yut, you would," I says, seein' she got cats everywhere: on the wall, one she even painted herself by number, two cat calendars side by side, and a whole end table of china cats, one is almost life-sized, colored dark red with eyes made of green glass. I turn to Jo and I see how her eyes squint and I think, *Yut, she's a cat; me, I'm a dog. Doro, she's a cat, too; Tappen, Beulah, they're dogs, like me.* Everyone seem to fit one or the other. Adele was a dog, Ida was a cat, an old one. Doro, though, she was a big cat, or a wildcat, maybe a bobcat.

"You know Doro?" I says.

"Yeah . . . We don't hafta listen to this anymore," Jo says as she leans up and stretches her arm toward the volume. "Yeah, a little, but Doro doesn't like me," she says without a hint of hurt.

"She told ya that?" I says, thinkin', *Yeah, Doro could.*

"Well, ya see, I sprayed her once down at The Old Caboose and I got her right in the face and she got all upset."

"Sprayed her with what?" I says.

"My tit, honey, with the milk in my tit. Why, back in those days Brooke was little, I could aim clear across the room, fill a whole cup. Anyways, Doro got up and grabbed me right under my arm, right here, and Charlie Stengle was there, well, I guess I was drunk, anyways, I said sump'n like, 'Hell, honey, you're strong for bein' so cute,' tryin' to git her to laugh and she didn't, she had me just as tight and she walked me right out the door by my armpit and to my car and she told me in a very sober tone, I better go drum up business another way. I said, 'Can't you have any fun, honey?' I mean, I wasn't that drunk but she sat me right down in the driver's seat and I sat there till Charlie came out."

I'm picturin' flat skinny Doro with milk on her face from these tits right in front of me that even without milk is 'bout twice mine, and I ain't small, and I says, "You musta been a dairy queen."

She starts laughin' and I'm laughin' and inside, under the chuckles, I feel a knife pokin', startin' a split, a tiny rip in my new life, my life at Tappen's.

Just as I start calmin', she looks square at me, still settin' in front of the TV on the red rug she got with geese flyin' off it like the ones Adele makes, drinkin' the last of her Miller, I still ain't half done mine and she looks at me through the whole swig and then she says after she swallow, she says just as gentle, "You've never been loved, Margaret, have ya?"

The way she said my name made me believe her and I said, "Nope, 'cept by a kid, if that counts."

"Oh, that counts!" she said. "You bet that counts. Yessirree honey, that counts."

"Ya think?" I says and I see her look down at my left hand on the couch and then I see myself that I'm fingerin' a cigarette hole and I don't even know it. Like a kid, I feel like a goddamn kid and I pull up my hand so as I can grab my beer with it from my right hand but it's too late, I can't help it, I'm cryin'.

"Bubby, he died you know." I kept snifflin' so it was hard to speak. "Course you know." Jo, she nods. Then she gits up and walks over to the headboard backa her bed where she got one of them shelves with a slidin' door and she bring me back a half roll of toilet paper and hand it over to me and I blow my nose so as I can keep goin'. I says, "And then I get Billy and I don't even love him . . . well, I mighta . . . but . . . Well, it don't matter, he don't love me and it's wearin' on me 'cause I still gotta give like I did love him. Bubby, I mean, he wasn't exactly a kid anybody'd wish for. I mean, he wasn't easy, he had *some* temper but . . . You never seen him, did ya?"

She shook her head.

"They done it," I says, grittin' my teeth. "They done it, they killed him, they dried me up and . . . We was connected . . . I mean, we was tied like by a cord and I done a dumb thing, I switched over, so everything I felt in my belly was really, well, it was him, it was his belly I was feelin' so it was me took on all his pain. This don't make much sense, I know. Adele, she thought I was wacko. But the pain . . . I couldn't tell, Jo. I mean, he couldn't tell he was dyin', he didn't hurt and so I didn't know . . . I just thought . . . I just kept ignorin' the pain in my gut, like all it was was a nuisance and I was gittin' real skinny but . . . It was them, ya see!" I was almost shoutin' now. "Rippin' us apart. We just couldn't be apart, we was just like that 'cause of that cord tyin' us together, and 'cause of me switchin' over. There wasn't no sin in that, was there? Was there?" I was cryin' thick now and she waited, a long time she waited.

"They thought I was . . . we was . . . perverted. But we wasn't! Bubby just needed to be with me. I mean, for his life, and I didn't know, I listened to Marilyn, I listened to . . . well, Marilyn. Adele, she told me he was cryin' wicked bad that first month we was apart, and how he sweat so, and my belly, too, it was killin' the whole time, but I gone on instead, like nothin' was wrong, workin' for that old witch, Mrs. Butler." My cryin' wasn't full now, just short breaths.

"It was them done it, and I go and listen to 'em, I didn't know . . . You know what switchin' over is?"

"No," she says real quiet, and shakin' her head, too.

"It's when . . . well, when you see from someone else or sump'n else, like a cow or sump'n. You see how they see, or with Bubby it wasn't seein', it was feelin'. I felt from his belly."

"You mean you can see from someone else's eyes?" she says, lookin' at me like I am *sump'n* else.

"Well, no . . . Ain't just with anybody, I can't do it just with anybody. It's bad, it ain't good, don't lead to no good, it's like . . . a . . . a drug."

"When was the last time? I mean, that you did it."

"With Bubby," I says. "I didn't mean to, it just happened and I didn't even really know it, that it happened, know it clear, I mean, till he was gone — you know, like you can kinda know sump'n. But ya see, when I was a kid . . . Boy, am I talkin' . . ."

"Go on," she says to me. She leaned her elbows onto the coffee table, toward me, her fingers was pullin' up on her hair, combin' it. I want it to light up when she pulls it up like that, but it don't, stays just as black as when it land back on her head. "Go on."

"When I was a kid, me and my brother Billy, we used to do it with cows. It was my dad first taught us."

"Do what?"

"Switch over."

"Oh. I thought maybe you . . . Never mind, go on."

"We'd be starin' at 'em, the cows, the ones would stare back, stare right into their eyes, and it'd happen, it'd be real quick though, just a second, and then we could see back on ourselves but we was big, bigger'n real, but then we got hooked and I could see it wasn't no good so I quit, but it was too late, I'd done it too long, so when Bubby come, it just happened, I didn't will it on, he woulda been . . . been normal maybe."

"Oh, it's not your fault, Margaret, you're just killin' yourself, you're just gonna kill yourself. It's not your fault." She looked square at me like I only been looked at a few times in my life and then she come over and set on the couch and I cried and she's sayin' over and over, "It's not your fault," and I cried right onto the pillow she got on the couch, and then she come closer and pulled the pillow from me and then I cried into her boobs. She took the beer outa my hand and she run her arms 'round my back, she had to lift up my arm 'cause it was limp and she put it around her so her arms could go around me and hold me and my face fit in 'tween those two worlds, they was like two worlds buryin' me, and I cried and cried and she held me, I was gittin' her shirt soaked and she still held me even when I turn my face like for air, she held me smack 'tween those two worlds, and I says, "I never, I never been . . . held . . . like this before."

"It's OK, it's OK" was all she was sayin'. We wasn't leanin' back or nothin' and finally we come apart.

I kept sayin', "Thank you, thank you," over and over. "You're so nice lettin' me cry and all."

"It ain't a sin to cry, honey," she said, and I think, *Ain't. She said "ain't" just like Doro, to make me hear.* But it ain't the same *what* she make me hear.

Then she says, "You're pretty, Margaret, even cryin'."

"No, I ain't," I says. I couldn't meet her eyes then. I stared down at my fingernails, all chewed.

"Don't, Margaret, don't" was what she was sayin' but it come to me like "yes, yes" 'cause she was rubbin' the sides of my arms.

I smiled and she started touchin' it, the smile, like it was no longer on my face, like it was risen, risen off my face and to her. Then it was almost like I was blowin' bubbles, I was kissin' her fingers and the kisses was floatin' right up and she was catchin' 'em. Then she was catchin' 'em with her lips and then I reached out like I ain't ever reached and I touched those two worlds floatin' there without a bra and I gone under. Under water, slow motion, under her sweat shirt, and I held her belly on both sides, it could move around so like it was full of water—everything, even the air, seemed water, I was gone under, and then I raise up with my hands and there they were, hangin' for me, they were so heavy like they was too big for me, but then the two nipples come out like messages, like kids playin' top of these huge worlds I couldn't hold on to 'cept if I got one of 'em with both hands, but the nipples, they were easy, kids, like Bubby, like Billy even when no one was lookin'.

I said, "I never done . . . I ain't . . ."

She just nodded like she know already and then she lay back and I pushed up her shirt and I come forward kissin' and playin' with her nipples and each tit one at a time and then both of 'em and the whole time, it never stopped, it was like water but thinner, rushin' over me and through me in waves bathin' me, and I was crackin' open, crackin' where I didn't even know I was crust, like I was all crust before and now I was crackin' and I was still alive like a newborn all wet still alive 'cause the water wasn't stoppin', bathin' me, and every time I thought I was all done crackin', nothin' left to crack, Jo, she would run her hands through my hair and I'd crack some more and she'd bathe me more.

And I forgot I wasn't good enough for love. I wasn't even scared no more.

And I forgot all about Beulah and Tappen keepin' Billy.

It snowed one inch, maybe even two over in Sweet Hollow though there wasn't even flurries in Langdon. The first snow, November 24. Every year I git the date. It was only a little, thank God, or I wouldn't make it up, but it was layin' on Close Crick Road just as fresh and it done what it always do, make me forget everything underneath and past like the world's just freshness and softness even with the dark 'cause all over the road what was just dirt couple hours ago was small shinin' bits of light.

9

Johnny

ONE NIGHT—musta been already middle of December—I come home from Jo's late. Billy was in with Beulah, and just as I was 'bout asleep I seen like a shadow of Doro slip through my door and walk toward the head of the bed, way her one hand is up front of her I know she can't see nothin'. She leans down over the pillow I ain't on and whispers, "I need you, come on." Then she turned around and left.

I git my jeans on, already got on the shirt I sleep in. I skip the third step down 'cause how it squeaks so and I grab Tappen's coat I been wearin' outa the downstairs closet, my boots at the door. Doro, she was givin' Breezie and Sam dog biscuits on the back stoop so as they don't whimper tied to the porch and us takin' off. The ground was froze up even harder since I drove in. There wasn't a lot of light, only a quarter-moon, and I seen Doro was carryin' a flashlight and two of Tappen's army blankets.

It was Johnny. He had been gittin' skinnier but I didn't think much 'bout it even though Doro seemed to be tryin' all sorts of things. She was puttin' half a cup of vegetable oil in his feed, too, 'cause his coat started gittin' these bumps on it that would scrape off with little flakes of hair. And she started usin' a cribbin' strap to stop him from cribbin', though she'd always said before that it didn't really help nothin'. Then today — she told me the whole thing on the way to the barn, her words was flat, comin' out one after the other like she was readin' 'em — today 'bout four, when she went to git all the horses in to feed 'em, Johnny wouldn't git up, she was practically kickin' him, and she called Dr. Hamilton right away, which ain't like her at all, I knew it had to be bad to git Doro to call a vet. By the time Hamilton got there though, Johnny was drippin' gobs of dark green fluid from his mouth and nose. Tappen, he done what he could, went to Agway 'fore it closed — Doro's always the one that goes — and he did the gutters in the cow barn. I left for Jo's straight from Ida's, I didn't know.

Dr. Hamilton gave Johnny a shot and then stuck a black tube through his nose down into his gut and sucked at the end so he could start pumpin'. I guess after an hour or so he told Doro to call him in the mornin', and Doro'd been out with Johnny ever since, tryin' to keep him warm, gittin' blankets under him as much as she could since she couldn't git him up. She seen the lights from the Impala, she said.

Inside the barn on a bale of hay was still a full plate of cold dinner Doro ain't touched — Beulah musta sent it out with Tappen. How she was talkin', seemed she was in almost a shock though I didn't know if it was that Johnny was so bad or that she had slipped — that he had gone down so quick and she didn't catch it, didn't know till maybe it was too late. I didn't know which it was but when she went to wipe out the bucket she'd been carryin' out to him and I seen all the rags there thrown on the floor by the pump, they was all bunched up with that green gook full of small bits of hay and grain never got digested, when she handed me the blankets and bent down with the rag toward the bucket, she give me a look made me swallow and blink, I knew the green was bad. Least he wasn't in the big pasture and least he was still takin' sips of water.

She took the light in one hand and the bucket in the other and I followed her out with the blankets. We walked side-by-side close, to fit into the light. We slowed up on a small knoll by the hollow apple tree Billy likes to hide in, we slowed up and then Doro stiffened, flashed the light back and forth. Johnny's horse blanket was on the ground, and two others. He had moved. Doro started to run, water pourin' outa both sides of the bucket, she was gittin' soaked, the beam of light bouncin' crazy.

Johnny was all the way back to the south side of the pasture by the fence, back where the deer go in and out of the barbed wire. His coat had gotten so dry, like a rug. He was cold, the air was cold, seem everything was cold, the blankets didn't help none. Doro gave me the flashlight. We both raised his head up and Doro cupped her hand and lifted some water to his lips but he wouldn't swallow nothin'.

Then he started to struggle, he was tryin' to git up but he couldn't. He was so big, sixteen hands, and he couldn't git up, his front hoof was flailin', makin' circles on the ground, he almost got his back legs under him, but then he'd collapse again.

"Margaret," Doro said, "you gotta go. He doesn't want you here."

I didn't move. I didn't wanna go. I held the flashlight out for Doro to take. She was lookin' down on him, his head laid out on the ground again, flat. He was breathin' heavy, he wasn't tryin' to move no more. "Here," I said, and she took the light but didn't look up. I left.

I waited in the barn with the three horses Doro was trainin' mostly for city people come up on weekends. I sat against the feed bin on the cement. She'd had Johnny since he was a two-year-old, twelve years or so. He looked so skinny, musta lost fifty pounds in just a couple days. I remembered, back when I was here pregnant, when I'd only just seen Doro around really, I stood at the fence and watched her walk out to the middle of the pasture to kill Cindy, a stout buckskin mare who had gone lame. Doro needed her stall for a horse she could train. Doro walked right up to her grazin' and put on her halter. Cindy still walked pretty peppy, though her head dropped when her left hind hit. Doro led her up to the hole Cliff had dug with his backhoe. She twiddled Cindy's mane with one hand and with the other punched her neck muscle once with her fist and with the next hit it was in, the needle. She attached the syringe. Cindy's knees stiffened. Took just her palm for Doro to push her over. One thousand fifty pounds, thump. I remembered I walked through and over to the hole while Doro climbed onto the backhoe and started it up. Cindy's knees had stayed stiff but her neck bent to the shape of the hole. Dirt was fallin' in, on her hind end, her back. Doro was yellin', "Move! Move!"

Johnny though, Doro'd take him up to the state land, always took a pair of wire cutters, too, though she said she never cut anything belong to a active farm. Stone walls she'd jump him but she never let him jump nothin' with wire. When they was leavin', Johnny would always stand at the gate just as still and pivot so as Doro could open it without gittin' off. And one time she had a fresh cup of coffee on the gatepost there and halfway through the gate Johnny stopped and Doro set there drinkin' it just as slow till she set the cup back on the post empty and they carried on out the driveway.

I sat there 'gainst the feed bin close to two hours, whole time feelin' Doro out there in the night. Then I heard it. Like teeth flashin' front of me, rippin' the night like lightnin', didn't seem human, seemed animal.

I ran toward the light. It was starin' a beam off past the fence into the woods where the deer come. I seen Johnny's eyes first, clouded up and just as still. Doro's knees was up under her chest, her head on the ground right up 'gainst Johnny's belly, her forehead flat on the ground. She had both her arms laid out 'bove her head in the hollows 'tween his ribs. They seemed settled in there, like she was tryin' to fill the hollows up, like she almost did. She wasn't makin' a sound.

I squatted down on my heels in backa her and waited. A long time I waited. I could barely hear her breathin'. I start to sing, like it wasn't me doin' it but it was right, I sing, real soft what I used to sing to Bubby, puttin' him to sleep:

> "Rock-a-bye baby on the treetop
> When the wind blows the cradle will rock
> When the bough breaks the cradle will fall
> Down will come baby, cradle and all . . ."

I sing it again and again and again just like Bubby used to make me. I start rockin', back and forth on my heels, toward Doro and away, toward that body bowed down front of her horse. I rock and she raises up off Johnny and starts to sing, too, we're both singin' and she starts swayin', she sways sideways back and forth front of Johnny's body, back and forth. His nose and mouth was turned kinda, lifted off the ground, his lips pulled back from his teeth, his teeth lifted up into the dark like a wanin' moon.

10

Haircut

"YOU LOVE DORO, don't you, Margaret?" Jo says to me.

We was just settin' around her place, 'bout to break open the donuts.

"I guess so," I says. "I don't talk to her though, not like I talk on to you, it ain't like that or nothin'. I just live with her, we just live next, side by side."

For a flash I seen that feelin' again, of bein' side by side with Doro, walkin' out toward Johnny in the pasture, seemed we was both just followin' the light and suddenly, I was almost scared 'cause I seen Doro, right there side of me, I seen and feel she was as ALIVE as me, like it never come to me before *really*, that someone else could be as . . . as ALIVE as me, seein', feelin' outa her side right there stuff just as REAL as I was seein' but different. Like 'fore this everyone else was just movin' talkin' toys front of me but Doro now, we was side by side, and then the world jiggled kinda, had to jiggle 'cause there was two centers to it, like the world was spinnin' 'bout two places now, mine was still a bit fatter, course, but there was huge spaces now all new, and cold, and then quick as it come I lost it, and the world shrunk back up to just me, a big circle 'round me, and I thought, *It's better this way,* 'cause the other, the other was eerie, made me want deviled eggs, how my mom made 'em.

I told Jo then—she was settin' on the couch cross-legged just like she was on the floor—I told her 'bout Johnny. "Poor Doro, man, she had Johnny such a long time. Course, she's the last one would talk on mushy 'bout a horse but, I heard this, I don't know, cry. And then I was with her, we was singin', singin' front of him layin' there dead. But she ain't once since then even mention it, she didn't cry neither, I mean, like *cryin'* cry. It's like she's . . . changed though. She's more . . . weak like.

"It makes me, I don't know, almost, kinda scared like, or I don't know, like the other day I seen her try to reach one of her girths she got up on the rafters, she was steppin' on an old bale of moldy hay and it kept squishin' under her and she couldn't reach it, she jumped up kinda to grab it, she didn't wanna git a stool or nothin'. I come in and I seen her miss and I bring out from the tack room this old three-legged stool and I step up and pull down the girth and I felt all cringed up after, I didn't wanna meet her eyes or hear her say thanks or nothin', I wanted to shrink away right then."

Jo just kept noddin', how she does when I talk, and drinkin' her beer. The TV was on but we turned the sound off. Whenever Jo's home alone she always puts the TV on real low just as background so she don't have to be in total quiet, she hates that more'n anything. I twisted off the cap to my beer and flopped down on the couch with her. That flash of bein' side by side with Doro seemed so far off, like a dream, dark, and real cold. I said to Jo, I says, "Your ma ever make deviled eggs?"

"Yeah," she said, chucklin'. When she laughs even a little,

her head and shoulders kinda bob up and down but her tits start jigglin' like a battery's chargin' 'em. She reached for the backa my hair, moved her hand down to the ends—it don't grow much no more, it's down to what my ma called my "wings," my shoulder blades stick out so. I love it when she touches my hair like that but it also makes me kinda sad, I don't know, it bein' thin and kinda straggly, I don't trim it or nothin'. I kept talkin' though, I said, "Billy my brother and me, we'd steal Ma's deviled eggs one by one outa the icebox till there was just the plate in there with the wax paper over it and all empty. Boy, would Ma yell, whoo!"

"You know, Margaret," Jo said, "I lost my kid, too. She didn't die or nothin', but, but, *I* lost her." Then she got right up for the refrigerator and she didn't say nothin' else about her, didn't even mention Brooke's name.

She was walkin' back toward me on the couch with a new beer in her hand and I thought, *Like Doro almost, how Doro lets on almost nothin' of her own hurt.*

"It's Christmas really that it gets to me," she said.

I wanted to say, "With Brooke bein' gone?" or sump'n like that, but I didn't 'cause I felt just the name "Brooke" would make the air snap. So I said, "Christmas don't sit big with me, neither."

Ida'd said Jo's aunt got custody when Brooke was just about four. Now she's six. "And just as blond," Ida'd said. "But it's a good thing Jo don't have her, with the stories she tells me." How Jo was settin' on her boyfriend one mornin', sheets comin' 'round her hips so Brooke couldn't see they was connected. Ida, she was lit up, tellin' me word for word, like she got it on tape, or like she was a minister gittin' it right from God, receivin' it direct. She starts movin' her hands and arms together up and down like she was treadin' water, though I was washin' her feet so she stuck her right leg out straight so her foot wouldn't drop into the basin.

"And Brooke would flap Jo's . . . she calls 'em 'boobs.'"

Ida says the word all hushed. "Flappin' her boobs 'round. Brooke would lift 'em real high up so they'd go slap as they come down, oh the noise they can make, Jo was braggin' on so to me. Or little Brooke would git 'em each goin' 'round in a circle, one goin' one way and the other the other way, settin' up a rhythm Jo would start drummin' to on her boyfriend's belly and all three of 'em would laugh so. Jo says they'd set there like that, sometimes for two hours or so. Now don't that beat all?"

Every time I listen to Ida, I can't help it, makes me wanna see Jo again. I start thinkin' how those boobs push up 'gainst that black bra she puts on every time I come over, and her clinkin' my bottle and sayin', "To Ida!" and then sometimes she adds, "May she rest in peace," and does a little sign of the cross over her right shoulder.

Jo, she was on her third donut. "It's good we're not watchin' TV," she says, " 'cause every show is a Christmas story."

"Yeah, Christmas, it just don't . . . I feel all hemmed. I mean, ever since Beulah, she set decorations all around, ones Adele give her in exchange for 'bout twenty poinsettias. My God, wasn't even the tenth of December she got 'em all up. Like I feel all cooped in. Billy, too. Yesterday I set a bowl of Cheerios front of him and he look up and he spit, spit straight at me. I didn't even whop him, I was so shocked."

"The way you talk, Margaret, he's more a animal'n a kid."

"Probably," I says. "Probably." I started drinkin' another beer she opened for me. "He needs air, that's for sure."

"Sounds to me he should be put to pasture," Jo said. I love it when she smiles, squints up her whole face. Made me wanna kiss her again.

"I need that myself," I says. "A little pasture."

Jo leaned toward my hair again, took a bunch of ends up in her hand. "You ever got your hair trimmed, Margaret?" she said.

"Nope," I said. I wanted to shrink up.

"Let's do it," she said, "right now."

"Now? You mean, you do it? Really?"

"Yeah." She jumped up, got a pair of scissors outa the knife drawer and a big beach towel and I sat on her one kitchen chair by her table.

"Hold on," she said. "We gotta wet it." She didn't just wet it though. I leaned over the tub, got my head under the faucet, and she washed it. She was kneadin' that shampoo into my hair so long my head felt like dough.

"Wowee," I says. "Does this feel nice." The water stayed warm, not like Tappen's water heater.

She cut off only the dead stuff, she said, but it was right up 'bove my shoulders when she was through, blunt. She was gonna make bangs, but I said no. "Why, Beulah and Tappen wouldn't recognize me, wouldn't give me Billy back." My hair felt so light and fluffy.

"I feel like one of them girls in them cigarette ads," I says. "In Colorado or sump'n." I was pleased as punch. And Jo, too, she kept liftin' the back up, fluffin' it out with her hand. We stayed there a long time like that, till musta been ten, just settin' on the couch, we never even turned up the TV.

11

Loader

NEXT DAY after lunch I git Billy in the car and drive right past Jo's in Langdon up to the Silver Ridge ski slope they put on Hide Mountain. It takes 'bout a half hour even though it ain't more'n twelve, fifteen miles. I walk right into the office and says to the girl at the front who ain't nice at all, I says, "You still need people to load chairs?" and they said yes, and I started next day even though we don't got snow on the ground, it's been cold enough nights for them to make it, they got three trails open. It ain't bad, they start you out over minimum. And Tappen don't need me much here workin', everything slowed down so 'cept with some of the plants that go through the winter, and I ain't ever been good with plants, seems, 'cept movin' 'em. Tappen always says 'bout Doro and me, he says, "You two, you're meant for animals, ain't the kind for plants, just ain't the kind."

I'm glad I got out, even though I gotta be in the car by 6:30 six mornin's a week, I got Thursdays off. They give you a nice parka, got a Silver Ridge patch on the chest, though sometimes it ain't cold enough to wear it 'cause when you're out loadin' you're workin' up a sweat. And every other half hour you git off from loadin'. Then I set in the buildin' which is heated real warm. Up there everything seems all bright, the people is all dressed up wearin' bright red, pink, purple, you name it — one woman come by, she had shiny gold pants, looked glued on, too. Danny Vrees, he says some of them suits go for more'n $700 and their skis is all bright-colored, too, and their boots, they even got 'em fluorescent.

It ain't that it's easy work, but they don't put a newcomer at the beginner lift, and that's where they got a lot of trouble even though they got it movin' so slow, or Lift 4 neither 'cause people gotta move pretty fast to load. The one of us ain't workin' the half hour usually goes on what we call "Jack alert," he's the head lift guy, and we ain't supposed to listen to the radio but we turn on WKRY anyway. My partner, his name is Roger and he's nice enough though he complains a blue streak and so I says to him, it was the fourth day, I says, "You ever had a *real* problem?" and he give me a look, but that shut him up for the whole day.

Sometimes when I'm settin' in the buildin', I start in my head makin' sump'n different from how it really gone, like Christmas mornin' when Billy opened the red cap I give him that looked just like Tappen's — I thought he'd love it, how he watches Tappen at supper, puts his elbows on the table just the same, hands fisted up front of his mouth — well, Billy give the cap one look and went right for another package but that was his last one, and he took off to the kitchen, sat right under the sink cryin' for a near hour he didn't git a gun. Longest I ever seen him be alone, he hates bein' alone.

Or sometimes in there, I turn off the music and just set and count the chairs go by, like my brother Billy and me used to count trucks. Or sometimes I close my eyes and the bull come up close and just seem to be with me, like he's right in the back of my head keepin' me company, almost like we could start talkin', like Bubby and me done when he first died. It don't itch at all then, it's real . . . comfortable, part company but part just me.

When I git home it's dark even though it's not much after five. I see the lights on in the house and barns and I hear the dogs and I feel I'm comin' home. Funny, you don't feel the word "home" much when you don't git out. And how Tappen keeps the house so warm with the two stoves, why, we go through eight cord of wood.

I walked through the barn to the back where I seen the single bulb hangin' lit. Doro, she was pissed about me goin' to the slope. She says to me—she was fixin' the feed bin finally after the porcupines ate the top off last spring, she had to make a whole new top—she says, "What about Billy?"

And I says, "Now Doro, I been takin' good care of Billy and just 'cause I been gone a few nights—"

"A few, hell! You been gone more'n you been here. And now you wanna go off days, too." She was starin' at my hair again.

"What's got into you?" I says. She been so funny since Johnny. She don't answer. She just keeps workin', she puts down the pencil she been markin' the plywood with and starts up Tappen's electric saw. I wait. I ain't gonna let her go.

Finally, she finish the cut and she look straight at me, she says, "You been hangin' around that Jo, haven't you?"

"Why do you care?" I says.

"She the one get you to load chairs?"

"Nope," I says.

We was silent a long time. She marked the other side with her pencil but 'fore she started the saw again I says, "It's the bull doin' it, gittin' me out, he was all cooped up and . . ." I stopped. I didn't want her thinkin' I'm goin' off crazy again, but when she look back up at me after she finish the last cut,

I seen she knew I wasn't and I seen she knew that I got the bull, too, that it ain't just him got me.

I says to her then, kinda soft, I says, "Jo ain't bad, Doro."

She turned away quick so I couldn't see her face but I heard her mutter, almost Tappen like, it was so deep, "Goddamn whore."

She walked out, her tools layin' right on the plywood she got cut out but not hooked on to the bin. The back spot was on and I could see her all the way to the house, walkin' over the path made mostly from just those feet walkin' back and forth. Just as she hit the two yews where the slate starts front of the kitchen door, I seen Billy leave off playin' with Breezie and run right up 'hind her but 'stead of grabbin' on, he just falls in behind like it just happened coincidence he's there walkin' indoors, too. He ain't dressed much, don't even have his mittens on, probably threw 'em in a bush after Beulah struggled gittin' 'em on.

Doro opens the kitchen door wide enough for both of 'em and lets him in first. Billy worships Doro. He hangs 'round me 'cause he knows I'm the one feeds him. *Like a horse*, I think, *just like a horse*. Doro, he knows does the ridin', I do the feedin'.

I wanna be a rider, too. I always been the goddamn feeder, the goddamn loader. I ain't never the one headin' up the mountain.

12

Laureen

LAUREEN IS Beulah and Tappen's only real child though she come just once to visit since I been here, back when Beulah was real sick. She's thirty-four and she lives with a man named Bart Waller in a trailer six miles up toward Witchopple. Debbie is nine, she ain't Bart's, she's Jerry Aight's little girl but he run off 'fore she was born. Tappen says Laureen always used to leave the kid here but since she started waitressin' nights at Maple Manor over a year ago, little Debbie's been stayin' home with Bart.

Laureen drives up the driveway in an old red Camaro fast enough to scatter rocks, thank God there ain't no snow, and Tappen come outa his work shed like it was fire. She jerks to a stop and just sets there, smokes a cigarette. I see little Debbie through the windshield, she's all wide-eyed and jumpy in a yellow-orange dress color of a dandelion. It's my day off, Thursday, I think, and she ain't in school. Laureen keeps draggin' on her cigarette like that was the only air she could git and even that was runnin' out. Then she throwed her body 'cross the seat and Debbie's door swings open and out she shoots, little dandelion. She don't even have a coat on and though it ain't below freezin', it still ain't up to 40. I see her dress got ruffles down the front, shape of a apron.

Tappen keeps walkin' steady to Laureen, watchin' his girl set there starin' straight ahead. He walks up to the car and Laureen pushes the door open, seems almost smack into him. She stays put though, smokin'. Then she gits out real slow and I can see, even from the kitchen window and with all that dirty-blond hair in her face, she's been beat up. She ain't dressed neither, she's only wearin' jeans and a T-shirt the color of rust. I come out and I can hear Tappen say, "You ain't goin' back, you hear?"

"Shut up, Daddy," Laureen says and throws her butt down, stomps it out. She sticks her lower jaw forward, then, "You stay clear of it."

Laureen starts walkin' toward the big house, kinda quick and holdin' her elbows, she's cold, and Tappen shouts after her, "Don't let your ma see you like that. She ain't feelin' well, she gone to bed."

Laureen stopped. She got her cigarettes out from her back pocket, started up another one, and walked the rest of the way slow, real slow like it was middle of summer. Tappen, he followed, but ten feet back. Laureen's jeans was real tight. She ain't as sexy as I figure she once was, how she walks swingin' her hips and then flickin' her head back and starin' mean when she stops for a drag, like she had some boy hootin' at her she had to swear at. The top of her thighs was startin' to spread and how she hunches her shoulders makes her belly stick out. She still got real skinny arms though, and the way she sets that one hand up on her hip, she's still got it, what makes the men come.

Her arms was all blotchy from bein' grabbed. Her face was puffed up on the left side and it was startin' to turn dark red, almost purple. She was squintin' more by the minute, seems. By tomorrow, I think to myself, she ain't gonna see outa that eye.

"Debbie's gotta stay, Daddy," she says.

I knowed right then what happened though I didn't have no good reason. Just the smell of it, how she said "Debbie."

"I come in from work, Margaret," Laureen finally say's to me. It was past ten, Debbie was in with Beulah, both asleep. Billy was out cold. Tappen was sleepin' on the couch, ain't nothin'd wake him up. Laureen and me was at the table drinkin' tea — first as she'd talked to anyone, like all a sudden we was best friends — and she says, "I didn't even see Debbie at first," and then she stares off for a while 'fore she goes on. "I didn't know what he was doin', leanin' right up against the bed like that over the spread and then I seen it, Margaret, her nightgown" — Laureen was startin' to sob, I could barely make it out — "in his teeth, had her nightgown right in his teeth. Holdin' it up in his teeth." The tea was drippin' right down her chin. "He got her, Margaret, my little girl. He got my little girl."

She wasn't drinkin' tea no more. Her elbows was straight out to the side, her hands in little fists up against her chest, 'tween her boobs. Her head fell in toward her wrists, little skinny things, her wrists, little bird bones.

"I seen them eyes of his, Margaret, I seen 'em. Like a murderer's, they was — killin' my baby. From the back he got her." And then Laureen wasn't cryin', but laughin', real shrill.

"He was on his toes!" She's laughin'. "The tops of his toes!" Her laugh got real weak, then it was gone. "Almost to his knees, he was. His feet, Margaret, they was splayed out like a palsy's, like his legs was nothin', like he was all arms, his arms was holdin' him . . . His hands and fingers, Margaret, they was white, they was spread out there on the bed, white." She was startin' to talk through her teeth now, her head sunk to only a hand above the table. "I looked at them veins popped out and it did something, Margaret, like I seen his blood full of dirt and I wanted it gone, disappeared, sucked up. I wanted his blood gone, you hear?" She was almost shoutin'. "You hear? Gone!" She was cryin' full now, her cheek down on the chrome edge of the table, she was gaspin' almost. "My baby, my baby . . ."

Then she stopped, just like that, and real softly, almost whisperin', she says, "She wet herself. Peed right there on the floor. And you know what I did, Margaret, after everything, after she was sleepin' again in my arms, you know what I did? I got down on that floor, I buried my head into the rug and I kissed that pee. I kissed it, Margaret, my little girl's pee.

"Then I washed her, she was layin' there in her red nightgown with the little flowers on it, her face just as smooth . . . She don't even have one hair down there, Margaret, not one.

"I found out then." Laureen's jaw set and her words slowed down and got real deep. "I found out. He'd got her before. There was no blood. I spread her lips and kept lookin'. Nothin', Margaret, nothin'." Her voice kept switchin' — hard, then soft you could barely hear it, then hard. "Her lips is so tiny. No blood nowhere, just pee, and the smell a . . . his smell.

"I ain't here, Margaret, I ain't here."

She grabbed on to me and I took her. Those skinny arms clutched me sump'n wicked, her weight saggin' her chair to mine. She didn't want me to know that she hated Debbie, too, in with it, but I knew. I felt it come toward me in that clutch of hers, her hate — how it come I almost saw it. Like I felt her nails diggin' in and I could count the ones was broken, one, two, three, four, and the others drawin' my blood up close to my skin. Just that clear I seen that hate come up and then fast, in a second, I seen her hide it.

I done it, too. How in a flash you hate what's dead 'fore you turn away, and that cold, cold laugh come up from the gut. Even with Bubby, my own blood, dyin'. Underneath it all, even watchin' him go, go on by hisself, underneath, that laugh come up and hold me steady, hold my body fast, or I'd've joined him. It's that laugh that changes you, that laugh that feels like hate but ain't, don't have enough blood for that — it's just same as stone pushin' up outa the ground killin' off flowers. It ain't hate 'cause it ain't human. Come up from below the chest, below the belly even, it come up from the bottom of your butt, rises up mean, sayin', "You live, girl, you live."

13

Bart

DORO WAS JUST 'bout ready to head out and hay the horses in 'fore supper and she sees Bart Waller's truck come up the road real slow, coulda stalled in first. We could all see, too, then, 'cause of the huge picture window Tappen put in a couple of years ago for Beulah. She wanted the light, she said, and to be able to see right out the back stoop everything that come up the road without even gittin' up. We was already settin' 'round the table, lazy, we was waitin' for the chicken to finish cookin', everything else was done — 'cept Beulah, she still wasn't feelin' well, she went to bed, didn't even want supper.

The pickup stops, seems on its own. Bart gits out and we all smell trouble. See, Tappen ain't let Laureen leave after she come here with Debbie a week ago. She don't know what's good for her. Why, she'd still go back after he got her little girl and beat the hell outa her. Bart's swayin', weavin' his way onto the grass toward the porch. The dogs was barkin' wicked, pullin' 'gainst their chains. From the kitchen Bart looked like he ain't shaved, changed his clothes, washed, nothin' since Laureen left.

Tappen's first one to stand, though Laureen's first one to speak. "Probably drinkin' solid. From the start, it's been liquor done him in."

"Nothin' worse than a mean drunk," Tappen says, his nose up against the middle of the three little windows set in a diagonal on the back door. He's got his hand cupped over the doorknob but he ain't touchin' it. Doro's up. I'm up. I got Billy 'hind one leg and little Debbie 'hind the other, squattin'. Funny, she come to me, not her ma. Laureen's still settin', facin' the window—she eats right side of Tappen's place at the head—she ain't budgin'. She's got both hands front of her mouth, how Beulah says grace at the table, restin' her nose right on her knuckles.

Tappen grabs the knob, opens the door, and stands in front of the screen, feet spread. Sam, he's calmin', but Breezie's still barkin'.

"You git yer butt back down the road," Tappen yells. "Ain't nothin' for you here."

"Yessirree," Bart says, real giddy like, swayin'. "Yessirree." Then his voice changes. "I'm gonna GIT 'er." He's shoutin' loud now. "GIT 'er!"

"You ain't takin' one more step, hear?" Tappen yells out.

Bart's eyes was like a animal's on the road front of a car. He was movin' toward the house in slow drunk jerks. "Gonna GIT 'er!" He's still shoutin'. The cold was comin' right in solid through the screen. I think of Beulah, how she's bugged Tappen two months now 'bout the storm. I hear Doro in the kitchen openin' up the basement door.

"You hear me, Bart? You stop right there." Tappen's voice has gotten real gruff. *Beulah must be woke up*, I think.

Doro's got Tappen's .22. Laureen sees it and groans. She flops her face down on the table, puts both arms up over her

head so as just her hair's showin'. The ends of it are stickin'
out funny, stickin' up straight. Debbie is curled over my feet,
her face flat against my shin. Billy's 'hind my other leg, leanin'
out from my hip, watchin'. Doro's past Tappen now, goes
right out the screen door. The dogs, they quiet, even Breezie.
Doro stands on the edge of the stoop holdin' the gun across
her belly but Bart ain't seen her.

"DAMN right." He's shoutin', mutterin', shoutin', mutterin'.
"YESSIRREE. Gonna GIT 'er. My girl. DAMN right . . . I'm
comin' to git 'er. HEAR ME? Ain't no one gonna—"

"Don't you dare," Doro says slow and steady.

Bart stops short. He sees the gun. It come over his face and
I knowed then what Laureen seen come into his eyes when
she seen him git her little girl. His eyes was glintin', it was
gittin' darker by the minute and you could still see 'em glintin'
with their own light, but nothin' good in it, weird light, like
the red neon over The Old Caboose. How neon makes the
dirt glow.

Debbie grabbed my ankle. My sock had slipped down and
I could feel my pant leg all wet 'gainst my shin. Billy didn't
move a muscle but his cheek was pressin' harder 'gainst my
hip. He was still watchin'. We was all watchin'. My teeth
clamped down hard 'cause I seen Bart raise up and he didn't
look drunk no more. His hands was out to the side and spread.
He was gonna spring. By God, on Doro. Standin' there without
even a coat.

He sprung and she shot.

Laureen throwed her head back and I see that dirty-blond
stringy hair of hers drop down on her shoulders, limp. Debbie
ain't moved, she was chewin' on my pant leg. Billy got his
face turned smack 'gainst my pants, holdin' on to my pocket.

Bart was bleedin' from just below the right knee. His jeans
was growin' darker quick. He was gruntin' in short spurts, then
he let out a sob but didn't sound sharp like, sounded dull,

tired, almost like them cows down at John's 'fore the stun gun git 'em. Doro was first at him, even 'fore Laureen. Tappen, he brung out a towel. Doro wrapped it 'round his calf, both her fists jerkin' quick apart to squeeze the towel tight. I turned the porch light on. The blood come on through the towel dark, though knowin' it's blood, I seen it red.

Tappen and Doro git Bart in the back seat of the station wagon so as Tappen could drive him to Cartsdale. Laureen, she gits in the other side by Bart's head just as Tappen starts up, Bart's head right against her tits. Oh Laureen, heart's dumber'n shit.

Doro slammed the car door shut. She starts walkin' back toward the house, head down. "Goddamn Waller!" I hear her from the door.

Debbie and Billy got the screen bulged out the shape of their faces, lookin' toward Doro. Most the edge is already pulled out from the frame, bulged too long—all the kids lookin' out.

14

Drowning

JO AND ME, we was drinkin' our beer — she had to git the Miller Lite, though she says it ain't no good, I can't tell — we was drinkin' our beer, watchin' *Highway to Heaven* with Little Joe, he's the star, though we wasn't really watchin' it, we was just what Jo calls "hangin' out," and everything seem so close in and easy. I didn't mention nothin' 'bout what happened the week before with Bart, or 'bout Laureen and Debbie comin' to the house and how it seem to take over Doro. I didn't say nothin' 'bout the .22.

'Stead, I was tellin' her 'bout Billy, 'bout how right 'fore sleep — see, he used to sleep on a foam on the floor but since he sleeps with me now his nightmares ain't so bad, he don't scream middle of the night like he used to — how 'fore sleep, he look up at me, says right out loud real words, a whole sentence, he says, "If bugga wuggas come and are bad, I just kill 'em." I gave him such a hug, boy!

I was tryin' to say only what's been good but I was tryin' too hard, I guess, 'cause Jo, she kept on lookin' at me funny, like sump'n was wrong or maybe just different with me. Then she got up, stood right behind me, and she said, "You know what you need, Margaret?"

And I says, "Nope," but she started rubbin' my neck as I says it, what she calls a massage, and I says, "You're right, boy, are you right."

She was rubbin' my neck a long time and then she started in on my collarbone, tryin' to pull my shoulders back, and I seen they been hunched, almost always been hunched, and when she pulled 'em back and my head back, too, it felt like my heart, it was naked, like all this time I been hidin' it. She kept pullin' my shoulders back, in like a rhythm, and every time seemed my heart was peepin' out 'fore it cower back in again. Then her hands, they gone lower, she cupped 'em right around my tits, first time she ever, and with my head bein' all the way back and my shoulders opened there was nothin' I could do but feel 'em jump right out, feel 'em grow right into them hands. She kept rubbin' around and around till I was 'bout crazy and she sweeped her hands down my side and come up under my shirt, it was my western-style shirt with the buttons that snap and they gone pop pop pop as she rose up and gone to the back and undo my bra and they fall right into her hands, my old nursers, hangin' down underneath the bra but happy, oh boy, my nipples was popped out like Bubby been pullin' on 'em. She took off my shirt and then my bra, she was still standin' above me and I says, "They ain't that big. Well, not like yours," but even sayin' it I knowed she didn't care and I didn't care none either, I coulda set there a whole day. But we didn't, we gone over to the bed, my shirt and bra still 'hind the couch where they fell, and Jo and me, we was playin' till she was kissin' 'em, too, my tits, and I arched back so hard I thought I was gonna fold up backwards. She started fiddlin' with me then, down there, and I was gittin' her sheets all wet and so I started closin' down inside like I was tryin' to hold pee in but that just made me git wetter and I was thinkin' how all a sudden it seem I was all hole, and all I wanted was sump'n to fill me up and I says to her, I says, "Jo, what do I do with a man?"

"Oh honey," she says, "you just wing it, just like you done with me." And then she started laughin' and she said, "I know why you're thinkin' 'bout a man."

She reached over to the bedside table with her hand that wasn't playin' with me and grabbed my beer bottle I'd finished and just as she nuzzle it down there 'tween my lips like it was a little chipmunk or sump'n cute, I knowed I was gonna explode and she shoved it up me and I closed up hard with my legs, even her forearm was stuck, and my belly tightened up hard, too, and it shook, too, and when I was able to say sump'n again I lay back and I says, "So that was comin', huh?"

"That was it, honey," she said. "You certainly came."

I says, "It's funny, ain't it? How it come on, like gittin' into a pond of water."

She was just strokin' my hair, not sayin' nothin', just listenin'. So I keep on, I was all bubbly, I says, "You know, like when you walk in and it's all tingly where it touch your skin new, but then how everything under gits comfortable again and so you go deeper and the tingle keeps risin' . . . Boy, did that tingle rise up, boy, till it hit . . . hit sump'n made me explode. Is it always like that?"

She nodded, but then she said, "Well, kinda."

"What about you?" I says. "You come?"

"Ahuh," she says. "But not tonight, I don't wanna tonight." I remembered then 'bout her business and I wondered 'bout the sheets bein' so wet under me and I wondered if it was really late and I was cuttin' into her, her money.

"OK," I says, not like I know what to do anyway, make her feel like I done.

She got outa bed and snapped her bra up again under her turtleneck that she cut 'round the neck so it ain't a turtleneck no more. Her bra snaps in the front, and she leaned over and scooped up each boob into the cup, and I was just watchin' her, and even though she got the heat so high you don't need no blankets, I git the sheets up 'round my shoulders, my neck even, all a sudden I wanna be all tucked in, I don't want nothin' to leak in or out.

That's just when it happened. Doro banged on the door just once 'fore she barge right in as far as the TV, and she says straight out to Jo, "You whore, takin' Bart in like that, you goddamn whore."

Doro didn't even see me, she kept right on to Jo in a voice feed out one word at a time, like they was each a bullet, "You tell me one thing, Jo. You better tell me one thing. Did you know what he did? You know what Bart did?"

Jo was behind the couch, standin' practically on top of my clothes. She got both her hands up on her hips and she said, "Isn't any of your business what I know. Now you get outa here."

Like Doro smelled me, smelled me there swirlin', my head was swirlin', seemed full of nothin' but vomit and she smelled me. Like she was a animal in the dark and without even seein' me, sump'n made her walk right over to the foot of the bed, grab on to the sheets with her right hand, and like they was a horsewhip, she snapped 'em. There I was, nothin' on but my pants pushed down 'round my ankles. I seen her eyes quick and then I look down, I look onto the wet circlin' out either side of my butt, I look down onto the wavy line 'tween the dry and the wet, I follow it right around, every inch of it, every little curve and switchback, like I'm pencilin' it right onto my mind and I gotta git every tiny bit.

Doro didn't say a word, didn't say nothin', she just stood there. Then she turned around and walked out, and after the storm door slammed Jo walked over, shut the big door. I sat up side of the bed, pulled up my jeans.

It seemed it wasn't really me talkin', though my voice come out steady. "You took Bart in?" I says.

Jo nodded.

"Did you know? I mean, about Laureen's little . . ." I couldn't, I closed my eyes.

She just looked at me. I went over behind the couch to my clothes. "Tell me," she said. "Tell me."

I turned around and looked at her, I was snappin' the buttons on my shirt. Her face, it seemed all puffed up sick, like it was all swelled. "You know he beat up Laureen?"

She nodded.

I gone behind the door to put my coat on. She said, "Margaret, don't . . . Bart, he and me, we . . ."

I put my hand up and shook my head so she'd stop. "I gotta go," I says. "I gotta go find Doro."

Doro found out about Bart from Jimmy Esker, the town sheriff. He drove into Tappen's like he was on TV. Like this was a murder case and he was the one, the main man gonna solve it, yup, with his fat belly hangin' over his belt so the last button don't shut and a cigar 'tween the two teeth he got left movin' as he talked. Laureen, she wouldn't say nothin', went and hid with Debbie in her room.

Esker says to Doro after he ask her all the questions, he says, "Don't you worry 'bout a thing, honey. That Bart's a bad lot and ain't a soul in Sweet Hollow don't know it. Don't you worry 'bout nothin', I'll put it right in how it really is." Like he was doin' her a favor. And like she didn't know that if it wasn't for Tappen takin' Bart down to the emergency room in Cartsdale, he wouldn't've written up nothin'. Then he says to Tappen in the kitchen, though Doro could still hear, he says like he's talkin' man to man now, so Doro's ears was already flamed up red hot, he says kinda low, "Bart, oh we can find *him*, that ain't no trouble. He gone to the Dailey girl."

Doro took right off in the truck soon as Esker left, even with Tappen more'n once yellin' after her, "Let him be, Doro, goddamnit! Let him be."

When I got home Doro was in her room layin' on her bed. She was holdin' on to the little book of sonnets her mother wrote, just holdin' it. Billy was in there, too. Sound asleep on her bed.

I opened the door real quiet like she was asleep. I walked in and just stood there, middle of her room. She didn't even look up. Finally I says, "She didn't know, Doro."

"You love Billy?" she says, like nothin' else gone on. She turn and look at me. "You love him?"

"Yeah," I nodded. "Yeah, I do."

"Ever told him that?"

I shook my head. "It ain't just me, Doro. He's tied, too, his ma and all, you know. It ain't just me."

She sat up, put the book on the table. Her feet don't even touch the floor from the bed. I says, "I . . . I'm sorry 'bout . . . ."

She shook her head and looked down quick. *They was tears*, I think to myself. I says, "Doro, I needed . . ."

She shook her head. She looked up, lettin' me see she was cryin', and she says, "Don't say . . . anything . . . Just don't . . . OK?" She put her hand up front of her mouth, her teeth right against her knuckle.

I says, "Since Johnny . . . died . . . you been so . . . different, Doro. I ain't . . . I ain't used to it."

We was both quiet then. A ball of hard quiet stuck right in my gut. Must've been over five minutes, me standin', her settin' there.

Then I says, "Drivin' here, I was thinkin'. If you was drownin' and everybody else was, too, it'd be you, I'd save you first. Well, after Billy, him bein' a kid and all. I'd wanna save you before . . . even Beulah. Guess it sounds kinda dumb, ain't no one gonna drown or nothin'."

She just look up at me. She says, "I hate that woman, Margaret, I hate her. You . . . Why'd you . . ."

She turned her face away from me. I seen from how her shoulders shook she wasn't holdin' her cryin' in none. I waited. I never seen her cry. She took some quick breaths like she was ropin' herself in and she wiped her eyes with her sleeve and her nose, too, and she looked at me, her face, it was all blotchy.

She was lookin' at me hard, lookin' straight into me, and I felt like she was seein' me again, like *that*, half settin' up, my pants bunched up 'round my ankles, my knees turned inward.

"Don't you see, Margaret," she said. She took a slow breath in through her teeth. "I don't wanna hate you, too. I don't . . . I can't . . ." She was shakin' her head. "I can't. I can't hate you."

I wanted to go up and hug her but I couldn't. I was froze right up in the middle of the room, like it was me drownin' and her on the boat. Her own little boat. And Billy out cold, he wouldn't wake up if you threw him 'gainst the wall, floatin' off, dreamin' back with his own ma. I move up to the edge of the bed and set down below Billy. I take his foot and swing it, back forth, back forth.

Doro looked at me, she didn't have no hate in those eyes, she said, "You'd really save Billy and me, before anyone else?"

I nodded.

Then she nodded, too. She took Billy's other foot and there we was, both lookin' off but settin' there swingin' his feet, back forth, back forth, him breathin' just as steady. Back and forth, like we was rowin' a boat.

15

The Old Caboose

IT'S BEEN THREE WEEKS and I ain't seen Jo. I drive half
a mile from her house on my way to the slope, or right by
if I git coffee and I ain't stopped. They was startin' to lay
people off at the slope. It's been a bad year snow-wise, every
bit of snow they had to make, and now that it was gittin'
'bove freezin', even nights, they started to lay us off. They
hadn't said nothin' to me yet even though it was my first
year 'cause they go by age, too, and they got a whole bunch
of teenagers and kids workin' and they was the first to go.
I put Billy down on my application form as a dependent
so I'm considered a family. 'Cause some of the guys was
laid off, they've been switchin' us 'round a lot and I ain't
workin' with Roger no more. I got hooked up with this guy
T.D., and even though Roger complained lots and he was
lazy as hell, he was always real kind, but come in this
T.D., and I hear him talkin' with a guy named Gary, I hear
him in the shack there on his break, even with the lift
runnin' I can hear him clear to the chairs, he's practically

shoutin', "Oh, you betcha, she plays Kiss the Pickle with all the boys."

And the other guy is sayin', "Yeah? Yeah?"

And T.D. says, "Right in town, yup, right beside the drugstore."

I almost hit one of the skiers with the side of the chair, almost knocked him down. Fire was runnin' through me and I couldn't keep track of it, got away from me so quick all a sudden I ain't mad, I'm startin' to choke up and I couldn't make out really why, it ain't like I didn't know 'bout Jo's— what she call her "business."

I had one clear thought then, come out like a shout through my brain, like it was fightin' its way through smoke: *It's more than a business. It's a kindness, too.* The men, deep down, they know it, deep down, even T.D. I can't look at over in the shack, he knows it. Doro don't, how could she? Nope, she don't. Like Beulah hands out food to kids, Jo gives over her tits, and seemed now all the same to me. Starvation. They both feed the starved.

I thought of Scooter. Seemed I was loadin' just colors onto the chairs. Starvation . . . The time he come over and how I ain't even run across him since, like God's been hidin' him from me, though I ain't forgot him neither, and I never told him when Bubby died, not before the funeral. I knew he'd find out, course. Miserly. That's what it was, holdin' in Bubby's death. Miserly. Jo, she ain't miserly, nothin' miserly 'bout her, like when she goes fishin' with her little girl, how she always brings Ida fish.

Last summer, Ida told me, she brought in a trout, cooked it up head and all, stuck a little plastic grape in the mouth, and she fed Ida at her chair and sat right down on the livin' room floor and ate it with her. She is *such* a cook, Ida says. Could git a job cookin' if she had a mind to, but she don't, don't wanna be tied.

Like Jo is livin' in the middle of a different world, and there ain't no right or wrong there, just some people needin' and others givin'.

But shit, then there's Doro. I come to call her "my Doro" though it seem so foolish since she ain't nobody's and never will be, she is *her* own, through and through. Doro with her little body and boy's chest, even at forty now, she could vault right up onto the hay wagon no hands, and it ain't just the spirit that come to her at night give her that strength, it's *her*. She takes one look at that wagon, then she lets her body do the rest, lets it be, too, to do it in its own private way. She got a secret, and with everything, not with just a hay wagon. It ain't a secret of words neither. It's a secret place she stands guard on, and fierce, too, like a room she knows she gotta keep locked so it'll stay always . . . empty, private. Funny, I come to love just that in her, sump'n I can't have and don't want to have neither, her secret, her inside locked up closed. Maybe 'cause she got a womb never had a baby.

Jo, her womb is empty, too, but different 'cause it's traveled, heavy, it's empty though, 'cause she don't let nothin' stay, she got all the leaks built right in.

And me, what about me? I ain't like Jo and I ain't like Doro neither. I ain't locked private and I ain't a thruway. And I ain't empty.

Beulah always says, "Never say no to no children. You'll never know which one it'll be to set you free."

Jo never says no to no man, and God knows which one it'll be start her car.

And I say, what, I say, I'm goin' down to town after work and see Jo. I say, I ain't gonna pretend no more I never knowed her. I say, I'm walkin' into that shack, I'm gonna punch T.D. in the face right now.

I guess I knew I was gonna be fired if I done it and still I didn't care, sump'n drove me to it. It wasn't the bull neither, though he mighta added a little strength to it 'cause I ain't strong, I'm only five foot four inches, 130 pounds.

T.D., he looked at me like he was seein' things, me walkin' toward him with my fist out front like I was carryin' a torch. He stared at my face like I was from a dream and not real life, and for a moment we was connected in that, 'cause me, too, I *was* in a dream. It was just a moment he stared 'fore he fell smack on the bench 'hind him, and I yelled, I yelled to Gary on the lift to git Jack, git some water or sump'n. I yelled, "I just hit T.D. and he's all dizzy."

Gary come runnin' but he didn't believe me. Though when he seen me holdin' my hand and T.D. just settin' there starin' straight off and holdin' his face, it wasn't bloody or nothin' but it was gonna swell, I knew that just by how my hand was hurtin', Gary, he said, "Holy shit!" and looked me up, down.

I said, "For chrissakes, git Jack." Gary run off and I lean over, front of T.D.'s face and I say, "Don't you ever, ever say nothin' 'bout Jo Dailey again to no one, you hear me?"

T.D. raise his head and look straight at me and give me as much a nod as he could though I didn't know if it was part shock 'cause it was a girl done it to him and he couldn't figure it out enough to even fight back.

They told me I wasn't supposed to ever be found on the premises again and Jimmy Esker was there, too, 'cause it was a case of assault unless I had a proper cause and all, and they was tryin' to give me a chance to what they call vindicate myself. They kept askin' me how T.D. provoked it, and they was all confused 'cause I wouldn't say nothin', not even when they said that it's confidential, to all five of 'em settin' there, and Esker, too, all front of me in the manager's meetin' room which ain't got a window or picture or nothin', even the front desk lady, never been nice to no one, was there.

Finally, I say, "I can't explain it, it's too long and complicated."

And Jimmy Esker leans forward, his cigar movin' as he talked and his mouth all black, he says, "You understand you could be arrested for assault. We got all night to hear you out."

I nod but I don't say nothin' more. Esker sets back and swirls a bit on his chair, we all got them swivel chairs, fake black leather, I see I'm holdin' mine tight, holdin' it still with my arms and feet like it'd take off swivelin' on its own if I let it go.

They'd already got from T.D.'s friends and a bit from T.D., too, though he gone pretty quick to the doctor's and then to home, they found out already that I didn't know him really 'cept by family, both growin' up here, and that we ain't spoke more'n two words to each other, maybe a hello here and there, 'fore T.D. come on the job this mornin' and that nothin' seemed to go wrong there. But since, how Esker put it, I ain't a known menace in the town and I always, up to now, been peaceful, I just got fired and not arrested unless, course, if T.D. wanted to press charges later on and not let it be on account of—and Esker give Jack across the table a wink—on account of "her long, complicated story T.D. might be more privy to'n us." Jack, Esker, all of 'em, they was all smirkin' and I left leavin' three days of pay.

I gone to Jo's then. I says to her 'fore I barely got in the door, I says, "Jo, I got in trouble up at the ski slope." I didn't tell her why, but I says then right after, "I got sump'n I gotta say to you, Jo."

She turned off the TV. Then she was already offerin' me a beer, like it didn't bother her none I hadn't been there since that night, almost three weeks now.

"I ain't stayin', Jo," I says, "and I ain't comin' back. But I wanna tell you that I, I, I'm really glad, I love that you're

alive and I never want . . . Well, I mean that, well, you're a
very . . . you're a very important person for lots of people and
I ain't talkin' sex neither. I . . . Oh shit, I can't say how I
mean, I wanna say, I want you to know, I think, Jo, you're
very . . . old . . . I don't mean physically, I mean like, Beulah,
too. It's like you're very old inside and that's good, I mean, I
don't mean bad old, I mean you're important just settin' here
watchin' *Wheel of Fortune*, you just keep on livin' here and
I'll be happy, though I can't come see you again or not like I
done, I can visit maybe, watch a little TV, but I can't really
git love from you like I been doin', though it ain't exactly that
I don't wanna. Boy, I better go now."

I seen tears in her eyes and I says, "Oh Jo." Seem like a
dream again. Like I been in and out a dream all day. She
shook her head and turned away. I wanted to say more or hug
her or explain more, but she shook me off. Like them tears
don't matter, like she don't matter, and that like everyone else,
I should just do what I had to do, and she'd just wait till it
was over, till she was all alone again and safe with just the
TV on.

I says finally, I says, "Come on Jo, now don't cry."

But by then, almost faster'n I said it, she had roped the
tears back in. For a moment there standin' at the door, I
didn't see her like I done all day, I seen her instead as just
a puffy-faced slut and I thought, *This must be the way Doro
sees her.*

I says, "I better go now, I guess. It's gittin' pretty late,
they kept me pretty late with the questions, you know, after
work."

"You got fired?" she said.

I nodded. I says, "I did a dumb thing but don't matter. You
take care of yourself, huh?"

Hearin' myself, I wanted to laugh and cry at the same
time, cry 'cause Jo won't take care of herself, she don't think

she's worth it and I seen that just now first time. Course the laugh come, too, 'cause how many times I hear Jo talk on how nothin' come inside her ain't wrapped in rubber, and no maulin' neither, they was her rules and everybody knows she'll stick right to 'em, nobody would try nothin' on her.

I says "bye" one more time and do a wave, too, and then even after the door is closed, I come out with another "bye" and I think, *Shit, Margaret, you gonna say "bye" all the way home?*

Then I answer myself, I says, "Maybe."

I keep talkin' to myself like I got a stranger inside needin' talkin' to. I says, "Where we headin'?" Like I got some place to go.

I says, "To The Old Caboose. I'm on the loose."

I crack a smile now, I don't even care 'bout Ida probably whinin' away, like I'm gittin' out, like when my brother Billy and me'd sneak out from Ma's, though now I feel like I'm sneakin' from myself.

Shit, I think. *Who's drivin' this damn car?*

I think, *Where is me?*

Then I come back, *Who gives a shit? Just go.* Only thing seemed real was the pain in my hand.

I get to Hazel, see the sign hangin' out from the door almost to the road. The letters just shinin': THE OLD CABOOSE. I walk in. It's so dark I can't make out the faces till after I set down. There ain't no other girl. There's a lot of smoke. I see Wayne, from the ski shop at the slope. He's smokin', I guess everybody's smokin'. And everybody's got beer.

The bartender's standin' in front of me. I says, "A beer."

"What kind?"

Shit, I don't know. I says, "What ya got?" and I nod to the first thing he names like I know what I want.

These stools swivel, too. Damn. I turn just a inch like

I'm testin' for seasickness. It ain't that bad. I go a full half turn. Smack toward Wayne, shit, four stools down, from the slope shop, hates you if you got money, hates you if you don't.

"Hard day, huh?" Wayne says. He hovers over his beer like someone's gonna steal it.

I says, "Yup, hard day." *Fuck, everybody knows already.* I push my hair back, I'm sweatin' like on the job. I got plastic pokin' me in the leg, that swirly red plastic torn and stickin' up from the stool, I pull some of the foam rubber out, git it over the edge of the plastic, damn thing, and set my thigh down on it.

I think of the bull. I think of the bull and giggle 'fore I even git a beer in me, the bull and Wayne together in one thought make me start gigglin'. I'm gigglin' away and I see, other end of the bar, a man with a tattoo coverin' his whole forearm is watchin' me and I keep on gigglin', I can't help it.

They're all locals I know, but I don't know their names. I seen a sign above the bar says, "No Knives, No Guns." I stop gigglin'. A basketball game's on the TV. A guy settin' three stools away from the tattoo man yells at the bartender, "Why the *fuck* we hafta look at a bunch of niggers runnin' around? Why the *fuck* can't we see sump'n decent? Fuckin' niggers runnin' up down, up down." The guy's off the stool, seemin' 'bout to show his fist but he's too drunk. His partner sets him back down, the stool seems to cool him off. The bartender barely even look up. Guess he's been doin' that all night.

Two doers here, I think, *and one, two . . . five, six watchers.* The doers are just too drunk to watch. Lucky they got the ball game on, not enough doers to keep busy watchin'.

I'm gonna suffocate. Now why ain't I up on some goddamn mountain like Doro woulda done? Here I am in The Old Caboose, been here since God knows when. My daddy, he

come here, a pretty regular drunk, probably even mean as this
here Wayne. I'm here in the fuckin' Caboose. *Caboose. People
bein' pulled. Pulled along backwards.*

The beer's halfway down. *Who's drinkin' it?* I'm hoverin'
over it like Wayne now. *Who's stealin' my beer? I ain't drunk,
though I could be, I could git that way, couldn't I?*

I wanna git that way, I wanna git drunk. That way I won't
mind bein' watched 'cause I'll be doin' sump'n, I'll be drunk,
I'll be ridin' the caboose.

I should go home, I says inside.

Stranger says, *Home shmome, you party poop.*

I says, "I'll have another."

Wayne turns toward me again, his belly almost reach the
bar. He says, "Goin' back there? Or did you git the ax?" He's
lookin' at my hand, I know the fingers are all swelled, I don't
look down at it, I set it on my lap, out of sight.

"I got the ax," I says.

I felt almost friendly to him. I knowed he could be nice to
me now 'cause I was lower'n he was, fired from where he has
a nice job, so he could like me now and I liked him likin'
me.

"Oh well," he says. "Ain't the end of the world."

"Nope," I says. "I don't care."

"All that money up there and you still end up with nothin'.' "

"I know," I says. "I don't need it, I don't need that fuckin'
slope."

Wayne come over to the stool side of me. Seems every time
I ever seen him, he's worn them same dirty jeans and that
light blue T-shirt. He sets down, gits his beer set up front of
him again, hovers again. "Almost end of the year anyway,"
he says. "Woulda laid you off anyway, soon enough."

He don't swivel none, nope, he looks off, out toward the
rest of the bar. "Probably never woulda fired you, been Christmas."

"Probably not," I says.

Wayne always looks off after he says sump'n. Looks off and drags on his cigarette, smokes definite man style, squeezin' that butt 'tween his thumb and forefinger like he means it, he takes each drag in through his teeth like it gotta reach that gut of his.

"They git you when they need you, then they don't give a goddamn. You really hauled off and hit him? T.D.?"

I nod yup. I says, "I really don't wanna talk about it. I wanna forget it, is what I want. It was a dumb-ass thing to do and I wanna forget it."

"I never liked T.D. anyway."

"I don't know him."

He takes a swig, then shakes his head while it's goin' down. He don't say nothin' more, stays hoverin' over his beer, watchin' out to the rest of the bar again, like we're together now and he's watchin' from a perch. We got ourselves our own little perch just 'cause we fill up two stools side by side, like we was bein' pulled on our own little caboose. And no one lookin' but the Spanish lady all painted in velvet hangin' on the back wall 'hind the tattoo man, lookin' down on us, must be Spanish with that hair as black as Jo's and her fancy red dress, lookin' down through the smoke.

The talkin' stopped then inside of me, and Wayne, he stopped, and I just set there, another hoverer, not talkin', not even thinkin', I gone musta been for a ride 'cause I had three more beers and I felt all private, pulled along in our very own caboose, just the Spanish lady watchin' and Wayne protectin' it, protectin' me with his back hunched over that beer, with his size, him settin' there peerin' out and not talkin', no one else was gonna say a word to me, and there we was ridin' the caboose together, this mean old Wayne, thank God for his meanness, scarin' away all friendly conversation.

"Wayne," I says, "you gotta drive me home. I'm drunker'n

a skunk. I don't even feel my hand." I hold it up front of my eyes and look at it for the first time that night, it was purple, the knuckles was all purple, and I says, "I love purple, don't you, Wayne? Don't you?"

He got up and took my arm and led me out. Everybody looked and one guy hooted right across the bar after Wayne but I knowed I was safe. I was safe 'cause I was lower'n him, and not just 'cause I been fired, 'cause I was a local, too, and 'cause I was already a ma, meanin' I'd been had already, I been poked. I was lower and he could drive me home and be a man doin' it, he didn't have to do nothin' else. I knowed if I was one of them suited-up women I load on the chairs all day he woulda got me 'fore we left the parkin' lot.

I got in his car. Left my keys right in the Impala. "Fuck it," I says. "Anyone want that car, they can have it."

"Oh Margaret," Wayne says. "That car been so good to you, talk nice to it now."

"Don't go gittin' nice on me, Wayne," I says.

He pumps the gas to git his car goin'. "Now where do I gotta take you?"

Maybe I ain't drunk. Maybe it can't git to me. "Sweet Hollow," I says.

"Shit," he says. "All the way to Sweet Hollow!"

"Yup, and my son is waitin'," I says.

He look at me like I'm crazy. Guess he knowed Bubby died, most people heard somehow. I give him a look burn out his eyes even in the dark.

"OK, OK," he says. "Sweet Hollow. Shit, man." And he pull out onto 209.

It's the bull in me the beer can't git to, keepin' me thinkin' straight, that damn bull.

"You know Scooter Hall, don't ya?" I says.

He nods. "Who don't?"

"He been keepin' outa trouble?"

"Nope," he said. "He was busted just the other day. It was all the way down to Clem Cove. Disturbin' the peace." Then he look over. "You two'd make quite a pair, wouldn't ya?"

"Scooter ain't really a fighter, he's just a drunk," I says. And I start up laughin'. Nope, I ain't laughin', I'm *howlin'*. I says, I can barely git it out, I says, "You know what . . . Ida . . . Ida Tappen done? You know?" Wayne was almost laughin', too, watchin' me. "You know?" I says when I could git the words in 'tween my laughin'.

He shook his head. "What'd she do?" he says.

I was comin' to a bit so as I could finish, I says, "She prayed and prayed it'd be Miss Ackerly git Scooter — you know, in school, fifth grade — and Miss Ackerly did and cried all through lunchtime that first day and Ida felt so bad, so guilty, she started up prayin' so she wouldn't go to hell, started teachin' Sunday school again, too." He was laughin', too, boy, got Wayne laughin' — just that was enough.

I didn't start up any more talk and he didn't neither. We was ridin' out The Old Caboose ride. I looked over at Wayne and I pictured his wife settin' home, and I think, *Me, if I didn't git hooked up with Tappen and Beulah, I coulda been married to a Wayne, too, with two, three kids now, fallin' asleep front of the TV while he was out ridin', ridin' his beer, ridin' women, and I'd be grateful, too, just 'cause that meant he wouldn't be climbin' onto me and he'd keep me a guaranteed privacy just because he was my husband and it'd be our pact: he'd stay off me and I'd let him stay away.*

Then I think, *Nope, it ain't just Tappen and Beulah, it ain't Doro neither, or even the bull, it was before that I was branded. It was the cows. They done me, made me different. It was them kept me from ever hookin' up to the world I growed up in.* And I says, "Thank you, Daddy," under my breath. "Thank *you* for my curse."

I was sayin' "Thank you" all the way home and Wayne, he let me be and I opened the door and the cold air hit me and I says gittin' out, "Thanks Wayne, I owe you one," knowin' I ain't ever gonna pay him back, knowin' it was important to him I never did, that for a man like Wayne payin' him back would be worse'n stealin' off him. I looked back into the car, 'cross the seat, just 'fore I slammed the door and I loved him for a split second.

Jo. *Jo'll take care of him*. I don't have to. I started walkin' up to the house. Yup, it's Jo let all the women live in their own private hole. It's Jo lettin' me and Doro be.

PART THREE

16

Gone

BEULAH AND ME, we was in the cellar countin' the dahlia
bulbs she keeps in the dark over the winter. Billy was watchin'.
Beulah spread the bulbs out pretty thick on the old patio table
down there and then we sat down and she counted one to ten
and handed me the bundle and I counted number of tens,
put a rubber band on each of 'em, and set 'em upright in the
enamel tins they keep just for bulbs 'cause they ain't too deep,
they're just right.

We was finished one whole white tin, and we laid back to
set awhile though we was just on the kitchen chairs we brung
down. I says to Beulah, I says, "The bull ever make you sing?"

"No," she says. "You singin' lately?"

"Just once," I says.

Beulah was just settin' in the dark, wasn't twitchin' a muscle
over there in her chair, even all bundled up like she was, she
was just as quiet, and then seemed it was her, her body just
waitin' so quiet seem to suck it right outa me, more questions
out, how Beulah gits more'n most outa just 'bout anyone. So

I says, "Did it ever seem you was a, a, doin' things seem . . . foreign?"

"Nope," she says.

"Oh," I says, and she was waitin' again, I could feel the pull. "Seem he, a, a, seem he ain't bad, I sort of even *like* him."

"I told ya so, didn't I? 'You don't know what he'll bring you,' I says. Didn't I say that?"

"Yut, you did."

"Just don't go off crazy again, scared the daylights outa me. Tappen, too."

We was up to three hundred dahlia bulbs, thirty sets of ten, and we had three more tins to fill. Billy was noddin' his head to Beulah's countin', like he was listenin' to music, or like a horse do, walkin'. He wouldn't bundle up like us. Beulah was even wearin' a hat and gloves 'cause of how damp it is down there, more'n cold, and her bein' under the weather so much lately, why we picked a easy job, though us just settin' made it colder. Tappen poured in cement over the fieldstone 'bout twenty years ago but it's all cracked now and dirt's comin' right on through.

Billy, he was settin' on a old sap bucket turned over, he was just glued, watchin' Beulah count out loud so she don't mix up, her fingers movin' like she was playin' the piano. Billy, he'd follow the bulbs seemin' to volunteer right into Beulah's hand, and he'd follow the bunch across just till Beulah'd give it to me, then his head'd dart quick back to Beulah. I started to think he was hypnotized, noddin' his head one to ten, one to ten in the dark.

That night I was puttin' Billy to sleep and he says, real quiet — it's the only time he ever talks, he don't go on gabbin' or nothin', mostly just a word here and there, like I call him Bing and he calls me back Bong, it was only that once, that first time, he come out with a whole sentence — but he says to me, he says, and even though he's right up 'gainst my ear, I can just 'bout hear him, a whole question he got, "Is ten the end number?"

I says back tryin' to git my whisper just as quiet as his, I says, "There ain't one, there ain't a last one."

He let out a scream! Like I shot him with a bullet straight through. I hear the door to Beulah's bedroom open, and so I yell over, it was just cryin' now, I yell out, "It's OK," and that, boy, set off a bigger wail. It took an hour, me rubbin' Billy's back and him lookin' chock full of nothin' but terror the whole time, and even after he did fall asleep, he was all restless and woke up cryin' most the night.

Couple nights later, it'd just turned dark, I gone into the barn after I come back from the store 'cause I seen the light on, but Doro ain't there. I finish off at Ida's and she still ain't. Truck ain't gone but she'd never take the truck if she gone up Black Clove, not when she gone alone and not tellin' no one. Beulah and Tappen don't know nothin', and Laureen, she was gone off with Debbie, probably to her friend Becky's in Kaatersville, she was gonna move there pretty soon, two rooms openin' up right middle of town, she wasn't gonna stay here.

After supper, when Doro still ain't back, I gone up to my room but I walk right down again quick and dress Billy up in the snowsuit I got in the lost and found at the ski slope nursery, and mittens, too, and I force a hat on him, even though he keeps takin' it off I make him hold it, and we git in the car and I think, *Why the hell do I care, Doro goin' off. Ain't the first time.* But it *is* kinda, it's the first time since I seen her cry and we was settin' there on the bed with Billy, and she woulda told me if she was plannin' sump'n up Black Clove, I know *that*, and how things been happenin' so with Johnny, and Bart, and then Jo . . . I head out Close Crick toward Jesus People Road.

I'm thinkin' the car's not gonna make it but I keep goin' anyway, luckily the ground bein' froze up made the road nice and hard, and Jo was talkin' in my head again how everything comes from luck and you can't worry if it's bad or good 'cause you can't tell which is which anyway. I don't drive it up as far as the truck goes but I do go clear to the end of Devil's Ridge 'fore the road turns up and it's actin' just fine.

"We're gonna start walkin', Billy," I says. Course, I gotta rummage through the junk on the floor for the flashlight.

We start up the streambed road toward what Doro calls the rock forest, which is just huge round rocks coverin' almost every part of ground 'cept where the trees are, and most the rocks are covered with moss, the green and white lacy kind was shinin' with the frost under — it was a fat three-quarter moon. It wasn't easy walkin', even with the flashlight, the only way we could go was rock to rock, real slow 'cause the frost was slippery.

I start singin' "Rock-a-Bye Baby." I think, *If the bull can do it, I can, too, damnit!* I'm singin' away, glad only Billy's there 'cause I remembered when I used to go to church, me singin'd make people stare.

It must be in the twenties by now, shit, the weather been so screwy this spring, and Doro out — even Doro can't take too much cold. There ain't a lot of light even with the moon bein' fat, 'cause it was cloudin' up a bit, too, though that don't seem to be makin' it any warmer. I'm wonderin' if I know my way good enough through the rock forest, I only been up here twice and that durin' the day, all through we couldn't see nothin' but the rock ahead of us we pointed the flashlight on.

There ain't no rocks no more but the trees ain't stopped and so I know we're off and I figure we're left, left of the — well, it ain't a trail, really, but—my hands were gittin' cold so I started shakin' 'em as I walked, I shoulda worn mittens, not gloves. Billy, he stayed right by my heels, seemed he was landin' on every footstep of mine 'fore I even finished makin' it. He wasn't cold or nothin'. I remember how Doro said to me just 'bout Thanksgivin', she said, "He ain't a kid, Margaret," and I couldn't help it, my eyes, they got all watery 'cause I was thinkin' of my Bubby and I felt, for just a split second 'fore I could wipe it out, I felt I was cheatin' on Bubby kinda, startin' to love Billy, and then I turned away quick, I said almost out loud, "No, I ain't." Bubby, he brung him, and then he done more, he freed me. Billy, though, Billy ain't free.

We come to where we shoulda come outa the rock forest. And I know then I can git to the ledges where the big overhangs are. Doro ain't there. *Above, maybe she's on top.* Top of the ledges, står gazin' or sump'n, outa the goddamn trees. We head off to the right of the ledges. *I'm a goddamn fool. I ain't gonna find Doro.* I head up here all worried and bullheaded, like I'm gonna save her. I think how Tappen muttered at supper, "Always sump'n 'bout Doro's doin's I don't know 'bout." I do know, though, she has a thing goin' with this mountain, that it ain't just a mountain to her, and after all that's been happenin', it'd be just like Doro to think Black Clove could mourn Johnny, Bart, Jo, everybody . . . Mourn 'em all outa her, she don't know.

We was followin' under what ain't quite a ledge but a steep enough bank so seemed almost a trail we was followin' to a place I know we can climb up. With the ground so hard, we can git a good hold, don't even seem our hands git dirty. I pull Billy up after me, and we turn around. Wowee! Seem we been indoors up till now, it's so open on top seem we just now come out first time into the air. The sky was split right in half straight over us, stars on the right, the cloud cover comin' in up the valley. The stars was so far distant and the cloud cover so close seemed like a curtain was bein' pulled over, like us humans had seen too much already and now, now there's gonna be doin's ain't for us to see. Billy, he was lookin' up, too, and he hung closer to my leg the more he look.

I set down on the rock ledge, wasn't too wet. Billy set down side of me.

I says, "Billy, you gotta talk to me. I'm gonna ask you questions and you're gonna answer. That clear?"

He nodded.

I says, "Why don't you say nothin'?"

He was lookin' straight ahead. I was waitin', waitin' like Beulah done, I wasn't gonna move. He whisper then, like he gone hoarse, couldn't git more'n a whisper out, "She'll hear," he said.

We was quiet a long time. *Ain't enough sounds this time of year, ain't no peepers yet.* I know Doro says there's a owl she hears every time she come up here, she even got the tree where he lives. But I don't hear nothin'.

"Your ma?" I says.

He nodded.

"Where is she?"

He don't answer.

"You tell me, Billy. Tell me."

I seen the sweat beads start glintin' on his forehead like they was little stars. I waited a long time, but then the littlest whisper come, he said, "Follows me."

His teeth started chatterin', he was shiverin' and I picked him up and set him on my thigh, I was holdin' him and his whole body, even his belly, began to shake. I says, "You cold?" He shook his head no.

I says, "Billy, I got you. I won't let her git you, hear? Now you tell me where she is. She won't git you, I promise."

He was cryin' real soft, but he stopped shiverin' so. He shook his head.

I says, "Billy, you listen here. Tell me right now. She can't git you now, but you gotta tell me."

He shook his head again.

I says, "Billy."

He barely got it out. "Here."

I close my eyes.

"She touchin' you?" I whisper, too, though I know it don't do no good.

He nods. And then I see he's holdin' his elbows. His arms is shakin' but his belly ain't.

And I says, pointin' at his elbow, "There?" and he nods again and I know I'm puttin' him in danger but I don't stop.

I says, "Tell her, Billy, tell her . . ." My voice is shakin' now, too. "Tell her to leave."

He shakes his head.

I says, "BILLY! Tell her to leave!" I was almost shoutin'.

He just keeps shakin' his head.

"Billy, I'm gonna leave you up here if you don't. Now tell her!"

I seen his eyes look at me in the dark. They was wild, they was filled with hate, he hated me.

And I feel the bull come, first the itchin' on my hand, then just *him*, I feel *him* backa my head like we was countin' chairs. The bull was with me now and I didn't stop, I keep on. I say, "Repeat after me, Billy. Say 'Mother.' "

He don't.

"Mother," I say again. "Mother."

He don't say a thing.

"Mom, Ma . . . What'd you call her, Billy?"

He don't answer.

"What'd you call her?"

I threw him off me and he rolled into a heap and was shakin' like a little two-year-old on the rock and I broke down, I says, "I'm sorry, I'm sorry, now don't you worry, I won't . . .

"NOOO!" I scream.

He was convulsin' same as my dog Montie done when he died, his little body was almost bouncin' on the rock and I seen his mouth was open and I seen his eyes, he was in a fit.

I scream, "NO! NO! She got him! She got him! NOOOO!"

And Doro, she come runnin' up behind me. I scream, "Quick! Help me! Do sump'n! She got him!"

I was shakin' him. I was shakin' him but it wasn't doin' no good, nothin', it was doin' nothin'.

Doro just stood there backa me, and I was sayin', I was sayin', "I didn't know she was that close. I didn't know she was so . . . so strong."

"Use the bull, Margaret," Doro said. "Use him."

"I can't," I says.

"You've got no choice. Now, Margaret."

"I ca . . . I . . ."

I rose up and I grabbed what I knowed was Billy's ma and I ripped her away from him and Billy let out a scream and doubled over into a little ball, his cheek pushin' right down hard 'gainst the rock.

He screamed and I didn't stop, I ripped her away.

And she was nothin', she was so little, she was dressed in a nightgown, almost see-through with a light blue ribbon 'cross the neck and lace on the sleeve. She was so pale, even in the dark, and she had skinny little arms. I says as I ripped her away by the hair, I says, feelin' it all matted up, musta been from layin' days in bed and not combin' it, layin' on her back, I says, "Git gone."

Her hands was so limp and she could barely stand and I says, "Now git! You're dead, for chrissakes! Git! 'Fore you take Billy's life, too."

She lifted up her eyes and give me a look and they looked just like Billy's eyes and I almost broke, I almost wrapped my arms 'round her to steady her, and I almost says, "It ain't that bad, it ain't that bad . . ."

But I heard Doro, she said sharp, "Margaret, don't you dare."

And I didn't. I says one last time, "Git gone."

It was first her arms that moved. They came up 'round her neck. Her neck was so long and fragile lookin', it was a beautiful neck, like one in them ads of necklaces. Her hands started squeezin' and I seen what she was doin', she was freezin' to death, she was shakin' and so cold, she was gonna try to squeeze her neck to die, she was gonna squeeze it but her nails, her nails got in the way, she had long nails, not polished or nothin' but long, and in the corner of my eye I seen Doro turn, she couldn't look no more, and I covered my eyes, too, like a kid, I was peekin' through my fingers like that would help but she was already dead, there was no air, she was blue and then she faded, got less, thinner like, till you could see right through her, then she was gone, and Billy was comin' to, he was still starin' off but he was comin' to, and he wasn't shakin' no more.

She was gone. *Shit, how do I tell him?*

I picked Billy up. He was awake but real weak, he couldn't stand. Doro and I took turns carryin' him. I didn't ask her where she'd been, and how she came outa nowhere, probably trackin' us the whole time, I didn't say nothin'. I just about made it back to the car.

Doro said, "I'll drive." I got in the passenger side. She laid Billy on my lap.

"The bull saved him, Doro." I could feel tears right 'hind my eyes.

"You did, too, Margaret. It was you, too."

I just nodded. I wanted to say, "Couldn't've done it alone." And I wanted to say, "Was it really the same what we seen?

Did me and you really see the same thing?" But I didn't, it wouldn't come out.

'Stead, I was sayin' over and over, "My Billy, my little Billy, he's just a baby, really, he ain't even . . . he don't even . . ." I was swallowin' hard, couldn't finish nothin'.

Doro carried him up the stairs and into my room 'cause my arm gave out, and just as she set him down on the bed, he opened his eyes though he didn't move his body none, he said then just as clear, "If you die, the numbers go on, right?" and I nodded and Doro nodded, and he closed his eyes.

Me and Doro, we both watched that line 'tween his eyes that cuts up into his forehead all durin' the daytime start to fill in smooth. Doro left after it was all filled in and I could hear the water go on in the bathroom as she splashed her face. I couldn't stop lookin' at Billy. His little face bein' so white, looks just like there's peach fuzz on the skin, glistenin' and smooth as a new pepper.

And I said out loud though I didn't mean to, I said, "If you could see me now, Bubby. If you could see me now."

17

Ma

IT WAS SUNDAY. Doro, she was talkin' to this man that called earlier, wanted ridin' lessons for his little girl, they had just moved up here, a lawyer with a big family, eight kids, wanted the little girl to keep with her ridin', jumpin' and all, and there ain't nothin' 'round here 'cept Doro ridin' what's called English. Everything's western. Doro says it ain't even western — "horse abuse" is all she calls it — them hootin' away at the county fair half drunk, racin' barrels and jerkin' them horses about, she says that ain't real western. Doro, with what she does, makes the horse do all sorts of steps, looks like the horse understands English almost, and always so calm, but ready, too, ready to do anything. Why, Doro's like a freak around here horse-wise, you gotta go almost to Westchester, she says, to find others do what she does — "dressage" she calls it. I says it sounds more like sump'n you do in a ballroom. Them jumps she does, too, with ditches 'round 'em, she does them through the woods.

Maybe 'cause Beulah ain't well, or just I'm gittin' like Tappen, I don't like it much when city people come here, more and more they're comin' to the greenhouse to buy plants for their second homes. "Makes 'em look so homey," one woman says to me. I was ringin' over $200 of house plants for her. Tappen don't seem to mind so much the ones come for his plants, but boy, he don't give this man a word. The man brung two of his daughters, the little one ain't a rider yet, just 'bout Debbie's size, stickin' close to the older. Tappen don't even say hello, gits out a grunt and points to the horse barn. Course, Doro talks a bit different 'round 'em, her comin' from educated folks anyhow, I don't know, they come 'bout noon and I got the idea to git outa here—bein' Sunday, Tappen could stay in near Beulah—git outa here, take Billy, too.

The Impala was deader'n a doorknob, and I started up the truck, I'd never even *moved* it before, I drove it right out the driveway.

"Billy," I says. "You ain't met someone you gotta meet. You ain't met *my* ma."

She was at Mountain View Rest Home in Witchopple. That's 'bout halfway to Langdon from here, and every day I gone to the slope I thought, *I really should go, it's been over probably three years now.* Then I thought, *I wonder if she's dead.* But I knew they woulda notified me.

The whole place is up on a hill with a huge lawn front of it and no trees. It was once a small boardin' house but it got added on to since the state took it and most of the old house ain't used now 'cause it ain't up to inspection. It's got a wonderful view of North Mountain and Orson Hollow from the front door, but they ripped off the porch where the old folks used to set when Ma first come.

The nurse led us through the lobby though it's only got one chair in it so it can fit all the wheelchairs that was lined up 'gainst the walls or just settin' cockeyed in the middle of the room. Everyone in them was in white or light green, looked like sheets, and Billy, he took my hand. All the heads was either thrown back with the mouths wide open and the necks stretched like they was baby birds or they was curled over, dropped onto their chests and mumblin'. I couldn't hear no separate words, the noise was comin' in whole, just a chorus of jumble. I almost bumped Billy into a wheelchair, he was alongside me, and I didn't say "excuse me" or nothin', I had to concentrate to remember these was people.

It's supposed to be all warm and cozy in there, the nurse says, 'cause it was a home once, like that means it's better'n if it never was. *Like them*, I think. *They was people once.* Ma, she's in the new section, all brick, put on by the state, in a room with five others, and she was what they call "up," meanin' side of her bed in a wheelchair. She belongs to the group got their heads dropped onto their chests. She looks the exact same as three years ago 'cept she ain't got as much hair so you can see through the white to most of her skull.

The nurse shouts, "Mrs. Becker, this is your daughter, Mrs. Becker." She's shoutin' so loud Billy got his hands over his ears. Ma don't lift up her head but I nod to the nurse so she knows she can go, and I set down on the bed and I says, loud as she done, I says, "Ma, this is your grandson Billy, Ma, Billy Hart."

And I says softly to Billy, I says, "Say 'Hi, Grandma,' " and he give me a look, and then he look quick around to see if he'd git caught 'fore he says "hi" in almost a whisper.

I says, "Speak up, Billy. She gotta hear."

His "hi" come out like a short bark.

I start shoutin' again. "Billy here come to meet you, Mama, meet his grandma." I see then why middle of her white gown is a wet spot, she got a slow unbroken drool right to her lap.

"Can you say sump'n to him, Ma? Say 'hello' or sump'n?"

She's onto a steady sound, don't seem like a breathin' sound 'cause it ain't got a rhythm to it, it's a steady groan come out with the steady drool. *The final sound,* I think. *The final sound she come to. Yup, she was steady.*

I keep goin' on shoutin'. "Mama, Billy here come to me as a gift, Ma, a gift. Not like we come to you, as accidents, nope, he come as a gift."

Mama lift her head. She don't look at us though. Her head keeps goin', lands on the back of the wheelchair, and the groan, it stopped soon as her mouth fell open, like she was waitin' for food to drop in.

"I'm Margaret, Mama, your daughter, come to see you with a little grandson."

Billy's lookin' all 'round with wild, bird eyes, but the only person seem conscious 'cept us two is a man in bed back in the corner by the window. 'Bout every half minute, he shouts out what seem to be, "Marble, marble."

Her head fell forward again, switched the sound back on.

I lean into her ear and my fingers, they touched her neck and a few strands of hair, and a shiver run down my arm 'cause the skin, it was wet kinda, and I thought, *Oh my God, she's alive!* And then into her ear, I says, "You got good company waitin' for you, Mama. I got you another grandson you can hook up with, don't you worry, he's a good boy, Mama."

Billy poked me and I look up and see the nurse walkin' in. I say, "Bye, Mama. You get some rest, you hear? Rest."

Billy and me, we git in the truck with the windows all closed up, and we let out a scream. We're screamin' all the way out the parkin' lot, clear onto 34 and into Witchopple, Billy keeps lookin' over, makin' sure it's OK.

"We're finished *that*, Billy, we're done with *that*. Done. Finished. Whoooeee."

18

The Bear

IT'S FIRST DAY of spring though it don't seem it 'cause it bein'
almost a no-snow winter. No snow and cold, and then all a
sudden first of March it gone into the sixties and seventies and
then it froze up, and now again today it's down to 38. Doro
says the exact day, March 21, is important no matter the
weather, no matter you can't smell it. That's how I tell, one
day I just smell it and then it's spring, don't matter to me if
it's March or the middle of May, it ain't here till I smell it
comin' in on a breeze. Doro says me and Billy should recognize the day with her, like she does every year. We'll go up
Black Clove, she said. She got her cow hair and everything.

I says, "Billy, you want a egg?"

He says, "Yup." My God, what I would've paid for that
"yup" a month ago.

I says, "Same as always?"

He nods, slides onto a chair from the side, he don't ever
move 'em in and out from the table. It's his third breakfast.
First was a bowl of Kix, second was three pieces of white toast

with Beulah's currant jelly she wants to use up 'cause the batch is from '78 — "This one's 'family,' " she said when she brung it up from the cellar. Billy's head is bent right over the table, he's fingerin' the little red and green boomerangs in the Formica. I have to say "Billy" so I can set the egg front of him.

All he wants is to watch TV. I says, "Nope."

I says, "Today, Billy, today we're goin' up Black Clove with Doro 'cause she got sump'n planned, a birthday party for spring or sump'n. I'm even gonna skip doin' Ida."

He's eatin' his egg I cut up too big, he has to bite off half a piece at a time. He don't seem happy but I don't care. No TV. TV ain't right durin' daylight, it just ain't.

"We gonna see a bear?" he says.

"Maybe. Doro says they're comin' back."

I set down with him, hang over my coffee. Since Laureen and Debbie moved into the two rooms middle of Kaatersville, I can just set sometimes again, feel my coffee steam up onto my cheek and watch Billy eat. His fork is straight up front of his eyes, he bites the egged-up bread off it like he's tearin' off meat.

I hear the wheezin' just 'fore the door opens. It's Tappen. He's got his cap on, though he ain't wearin' a coat, just his red sweat shirt zips up the front I ain't seen since last year. Course, it ain't red no more in the front 'cause of all the grease it got on it. He stands there front of the door. I says, "You want coffee?" He shakes his head. He wants work, is what he wants, outa me. Outdoors, even though I been takin' over Beulah's place whenever she's been stayin' in bed.

I says, "We're goin' with Doro."

"See she's made you as sour on real work as she gone, huh?" He turns 'round and heads out to the horse barn, I know, to find Doro — "a visitor in a horse barn," he calls hisself, "a goddamn tourist." I can hear him wheezin' almost all the way. When Beulah's in bed durin' the daylight, Tappen wheezes. It's like a motor you can count on.

I git up and take a shepherd's pie out of the freezer to thaw. Ain't no trouble to put that in the oven if we ain't back in time to git supper.

Billy don't wanna wear a jacket or the work boots Adele give us. I say, "Fifty-fifty." He picks the boots. They're just like Tappen's and so they're OK even if I was the one told him to wear 'em. I should've told him *not* to wear a jacket, it ain't easy to remember though, puttin' everything backwards. We meet Doro out in the barn dumpin' up fresh bags of Trim and crushed oats into the feed bin. Ooh, the smell of that Trim, like pure molasses.

"We're not goin'," she says. "Tappen needs help rototillin' and —"

"That ain't ever stopped you before," I says. "'Sides, it's three weeks at least 'fore we gonna plant any peas."

"I know, I know. But, Beulah in bed and all, we can go some . . . I just, I just don't . . ." She's shakin' her head.

"OK, OK," I says. "I ain't pressurin' ya. I got shepherd's pie outa the freezer so as we don't have to cook." I says "we" but Doro ain't ever cooked a day in her life.

She look up from her shovel, "Why don't you two go?" she says. "Tappen, he really just needs one of us and you'd be with Billy lots anyway."

"Go up Black Clove, you mean?"

"Yeah, you and Billy."

"I wouldn't know what to do up there, I don't have nothin' goin' with that mountain. Or spring comin' neither."

"Just go up there. Take Billy up there."

Billy, he's off in the first corral outside the barn. It's small, mostly dirt and filled with horseshit Doro tries to keep cleaned up so she can do some of her trainin' there, all the circlin' she does on the horses, canterin' one way, then the other. Billy's swingin' his arm, sword fightin' his "tend" friends, he calls 'em — he don't say the "pre" — there's bad ones and good ones, they even got a leader. He's got green all over them boots we only got four days ago. Dogs and kids, they're a goddamn magnet to horseshit, but at least he ain't eatin' it.

I says, "Was you plannin' some voodoo up there or sump'n?" Doro laughed. "Oh Margaret, just head up there!"

"Well," I says, "OK, I'll drive up there with Billy, I guess . . . Since you're freein' me up for the day, might as well."

I yell for Billy and walk out toward the house to pack up some peanut butter and jelly. I turn around and see Doro's in the doorway lookin' at me, hair flamed up, and she got that grin on her like the first time I ever seen her, that grin run side to side 'cross her whole face.

Billy and me git in the Impala. I think of Jo 'cause the car is down to a fifty-fifty chance of startin', too. I turn the key, pump it, and yell, "Come on come on come on come on," fast as I can and it starts.

'Fore we even git out the driveway, we start singin'. Well, we don't actually *sing*, really, we sort of croon and shout and yell, and I act like I'm Frank Sinatra or some fancy opera singer, or like this time Billy wanted the Bread and Butter song. It ain't much but we like it, Billy's Butter and I'm Bread, and Bread wants Butter and Butter wants Bread, and we can go on forever like that back and forth pretendin' we got microphones and everything, I put the ohs and ahs in and Billy, sometimes he sounds just like a drum, butter butter butter butter butter butter.

We're singin' away and I see Jesus People Road and I just pass it, I don't turn up, I go on by. Just as simple.

"Well, Billy," I says. "I guess we ain't goin' up Black Clove." I felt like Christopher Columbus, drivin' right over Witchopple Mountain and into Langdon, only when I turned right at the slope, I knowed where I was headin'. There was only a few cars in the parkin' lot, they was closed probably till the weekend. It ain't just that a lot of snow melted and what didn't is all brownish, but when it gits so hot early on, almost 75 the beginnin' of March, the people don't come no more even if it gits cold again and even though there's more snow than in the fall when they was swarmin' here. "Playin' tennis," Jack, our boss, once said. "They're all off playin' tennis or in Colorado."

I drove all the way over to the west side of the parkin' lot, where they made the employees park till it got so muddy over there they had to git a tow truck to pull some of us out, and then they changed the rule and let us park with the public. It's far enough away so no one can see you, and there ain't no houses this side, and Billy and me, we headed straight up through the beginner part of the mountain on the side of the ski trail where there ain't no snow but it's clear so it's easier walkin' than in the woods. I had three sandwiches stuck in my jacket and any minute I was expectin' Billy to set right down and quit.

He didn't though. We got to the top of the first beginner's slope and headed into the woods that was all ledgy and wet, and I knowed then I was actually gonna try to bring Billy all the way up to the caves where I gone with my daddy back when I was eight years old. I could still see the bottom of Lift 5 before we got sucked into the woods and there was hay all 'round the ground where the people stand in line so they don't have to walk on dirt and git their skis ruined. I thought, *This is still Hide Mountain, it ain't all Silver Ridge and second homes yet, it's still where I seen my first bear.*

I says, "Billy, we gotta go straight up. You can do it, you're big enough. We're gonna see a bear."

He ain't complainin', keeps followin' me, but I ain't easy 'bout it. He ain't the whinin' type, he's worse. He just sets down when he gits mad, lets out a scream. Closes right up. Ain't nothin'll git through then.

We walked only 'bout a hundred yards in the woods over mostly dead leaves — little pines, logs, we was avoidin' the ledgy parts — 'fore we hit a road, looks just like a loggin' road but it got tracks from the Sno-Cats they drive up and down. It ends in what people call Easy Street, one of the easiest trails come from the top.

A ski patrolman — I can tell by the parka — is comin' 'round the curve probably three hundred yards up, carryin' a bunch of bamboo poles all painted orange. He got a partner, too, one don't have skis on and wearin' just a T-shirt, walkin' to the side of the skinny track of snow, pickin' up the poles from the dirt and handin' 'em over to him. Must be bringin' 'em in for the season. The patrolman keeps pickin' his way down, some places he walks with his skis straight over the mud parts. We stay backa two trees edge of the woods, peekin' out as they go by. Billy, he feels like we're doin' sump'n scary illegal so he gits all excited, hunchin' his shoulders up and goin' buggy-eyed.

We go back out to the trail after they gone by so as it'd be easier, we got so much farther to go to git to the caves and I can't see us bushwhackin' the whole way, it'd take all day, might even now with Billy's pace. We got up to the midpoint of the mountain where a road goes clear 'cross the whole area through every trail. There wasn't no snow in the woods and the thin little line of snow down Easy Street looked like a streak of sump'n ugly, sump'n ain't s'posed to be there, like mascara drippin' down on Jo when she sweats too hard.

We headed back into the woods at the next corner after the midpoint so we could head to the left. They was all wet leaves and logs we had to climb over and I thought, *We ain't ever gonna git to the caves*. I didn't even know if I could remember where they was, probably we was up only twenty-three, twenty-five hundred feet, we had another five hundred feet at least to go, since with all the leaves off, you can see on the mountain drivin' in from the Hazel side, you can see where the rocks jut out that got the caves under 'em, 'bout three quarters of the way to the top.

I think of Daddy. How I used to talk on to him 'fore Bubby died. And I says right out loud, I says, "Daddy," but he ain't there. I can just imagine him after Bubby died, thinkin', "One on this side is enough, by God, don't want my girl talkin' to a crowd." Oh Daddy, wish you'd pull Ma along, but I know it ain't like that. Ain't ever like a kid wants

Nope, Daddy ain't around and neither is the bear. Probably no bear been seen up here, even by the caves, for fifteen years, all the bustle. Oh Billy, we're on the lookout for sump'n ain't here. I drag you up a mountain and it ain't here. There ain't nothin' to show you, nothin' to look for neither.

"Billy," I say, "we'll just go as high as we can, just git close to 'em, the caves at least."

Billy set down.

"You got the right idea," I says and set down, too. "You wanna sandwich?"

He shake his head. "We gonna see a bear?" he says.

"I know I told ya, Billy, I seen a bear here when I was walkin' with my daddy, 'bout your . . . but you know he . . ."

I couldn't finish. We set there awhile not talkin'. We ain't even in the ballpark of the caves and the sweat is just pourin' off both of us, even Billy with only a shirt on.

"How many is he?" Billy asked.

"The bear?" I says.

Billy nods.

"Oh. Ah . . . I don't . . . probably twenty."

"That many as Beulah?"

"Older," I says. "In bear years."

He don't say nothin'.

I says, "Billy, he ain't gonna be here. I'm sorry. He ain't gonna be here. We could still go up to the caves but ain't no bear here. I'm sorry."

"He's dead, you mean?"

"I don't know. But he ain't here anyway. The bear, they've all gone off this mountain, too many people and stuff, the ski slope. You mad at me draggin' you up here?"

He shook his head. Then he got up and headed the way he was facin', down. I followed him, lookin' down on him. We didn't say nothin', we was goin' down slow, I stayed behind him the whole way, all the way till we hit the car.

"You want any ice cream?" I says as I start the motor.

Billy nods.

"OK," I says. "Ice cream it is. The Tasty Swirl it is."

Tasty Swirl wasn't open yet, another month, but Jimmy's had some hard ice cream and we both had white, how Billy calls it, and we clunked 'em together and Billy almost come out with a laugh 'cause they kinda stuck but didn't make no noise and I says, "To spring, Billy! To the first ice cream of the spring! Yup, you tell Doro now, we done our — what she calls her solstice thing. You tell her, yup, we done our spring dues." Billy was smilin', lickin' his cone, and I says underneath, private, I says, "To the bear."

Billy was turnin' the cone and lickin' all 'round it from the bottom up, wasn't one drip.

"Don't have to teach you nothin' 'bout eatin' ice cream. That ain't gonna git away from you, no sirree, nothin' there to show you."

19

Porcupines

WE'RE IN ONE of the worse porcupine seasons this place ever seen, accordin' to Tappen. In less than a week they ate the fuel line to the truck, ate the bottom of three railin's on the porch, ate all hell in the barn, even started on one of the tractor tires. Most years Tappen, he parks hisself in the cow barn with his .22 'bout three nights end of April or early May, and in just them nights he can git close to twenty. "Takes care of 'em for a while," he says. "At least till the next spring. Maybe we got one or two after that but not a whole army."

Tappen ain't done it this year 'cause he don't wanna leave Beulah middle of the night. She's been callin' out to him, needin' help gittin' to the bathroom, and Wednesday night she even needed a basin. So I says to Tappen—it was after supper, we was eatin' spumoni ice cream, his favorite, we was tryin' to cheer him up—I says to him, "I'll stay out, Tappen, and kill them porcupines though you know I never shot a gun."

I don't need no gun, Tappen says. I can learn Kruppy Cole style. "Why, he used to go up Black Point with just a potato hook and come home in four hours carryin' ten, fifteen porcupines over his shoulder hangin' on the handle. He'd tie 'em up by their feet, got fifty cents a head for each one of 'em."

Kruppy Cole style means gittin' the back of the porcupine's neck with the potato hook (it don't dig into him at all on account of the quills), then draggin' him out to where he's right front of you, and then quick as nothin', flippin' the potato hook over and smackin' him on the end of the nose with the back of it. That's the most important thing, Tappen says. The only way to kill a porcupine is on the end of the nose, smack on the end.

Billy says he's gonna set out with me.

I says, "Billy, it ain't gonna be fun out there. It ain't gonna be like a party."

He don't say nothin'.

"OK," I says, "you can come, but there ain't gonna be nothin' but settin' up watchin' and then gittin' 'em. Nothin' else, hear?"

He nods.

We was in our room, Billy and me, I wanted Billy to take a nap 'fore we gone out. I was gittin' him in a sweat shirt so as I wouldn't have to change him later, he can't git it over his head by hisself 'cause the neck is too tight, and I wanted the big socks on him he has to wear to make the work boots Adele give him fit.

Doro come, lean on the door frame. She says, "Margaret, thanks. I know you don't wanna do it either."

"Ehn," I says, twistin' 'round from Billy's socks. "It ain't that big a deal for me and, you know . . . I just thought, well, seem better if I do it, ain't a big deal." Ever since I seen Doro bow down front of that dead horse of hers, I seen her different, like she ain't the same Doro I seen stick that needle into a mare's neck and barely blink doin' it. "Can't keep a lame horse," is what she'd said, and now, here I am keepin' her from havin' to kill a damn porcupine. "It ain't a big deal," I says again. I had to turn back around and twist the tube socks straight, so the toe seams are perfectly straight, otherwise Billy hollers, "My foot! My foot!" when he puts on his shoe, like a nail got in there. I call him then the princess with the pea.

"You sure you wanna go, Billy?" Doro says.

"Yup," Billy says, noddin' like a horse that needs a martingale.

"Margaret, you know Beulah's worse than I thought. Tomorrow she's gonna see Dr. Brigham."

"Really?" I says. "Beulah is?" I set down on the bed with a flop. "Really? She's goin' to a doctor?"

"You been thinkin' about it at all? You know she isn't just under the weather. It ain't the summer flu she got."

Damn Doro. "I know," I says, but it come out hard, a wall shoot up 'tween us. "Course I been thinkin' 'bout it."

"Well?" she says.

"Well, I have but, it ain't . . . I can't talk about it now, OK Doro?" I didn't look at her, I twisted 'round to pull back the blankets so as Billy could scoot under 'em.

"OK," she said, and I heard her walk down the hall and open her door, she always leaves it shut, not me, make the air all stuffy.

I give Billy a kiss even though he pretends he don't like it, shrinks back like it tickles, he can't help smilin' though. The light seem eerie, like the one time Billy, my brother, shook me up four in the mornin' 'cause we was travelin' to our grandparents' 'fore Grandma die, and they was out to Cherry Valley, past Cobleskill, last time our family ever gone anywhere, and I remember layin' in bed watchin' all the bustle down the hall. Ma, she was packin' and Daddy was yellin' at Sharon for puttin' make-up on in the bathroom. I was the last up 'cause I was the youngest, I was 'bout nine, I guess. I was layin' there with the blankets up 'round my shoulders, lookin' at the light. It didn't seem same as light turned on 'fore bed. There wasn't no mornin' comin' in yet neither, but still, the lights on didn't seem same color, they was yellower, eerie. Almost make a shiver run through me. Seemed that way now though it was only nine-thirty and I rubbed Billy's back and his arms fast how he likes it till by his breathin' seem he drifted off. I shoulda waited half a minute more 'cause when I stopped he opened his eyes wide and I had to start up again, I counted all the way to 150 with even the thousand in between till I knowed he was definitely out.

I took a nap, too, till around eleven-thirty. I woke Billy. He put his foot down on each stair so careful, I say, "Billy, we ain't stealin' jewels or nothin'." Course, he don't want a jacket, but I say, "No jacket, you don't come." I wasn't gonna be chasin' back into the house when he start shiverin'. But it was the warmest night yet of the spring, air felt almost like summer. I done like Doro and give the dogs some biscuits so they don't make a fuss and wake the rest up. I grabbed the potato hook right by the door, Tappen got it for me from the field shed soon as he finished his bowl of ice cream. The ground was so soft we thought we was leavin' tracks. Billy had his boots on, thank God, or his feet'd be wet all night. With the heavy dew and it bein' so warm, smelled like things was loosenin' up in the ground, rumblin' down under and givin' off that smell, spring smell.

The best place to git the porcupines, Tappen said, was in the cow barn, now the cows were out to pasture. We'd start there, I figured, but one night I better stay out in the horse barn, that's been hit pretty bad, too, Doro's got her tack hangin' up on the rafters. Billy had the flashlight. He was dyin' to turn it on, he just loves turnin' on and off lights, controllin' lights.

(Once even durin' supper all a sudden we was in the dark. He drove us all crazy for a week till Tappen put an end to it.) I said, "Wait till we hit the barn, Billy." It'd be treacherous walkin' without light in the barn. It ain't just findin' the aisles, Tappen ain't what you call a neatnik, he's an all-out slob, got sump'n every six feet 'round here, inside and out, and he don't believe in throwin' nothin' away neither, he makes savin' things a religion.

We set down right across from where the milk house connects to the main barn, 'cause that's 'bout middle of the barn and there's a light switch right there Billy can reach and 'bout six, seven bales of hay been thrown down from above 'bout two weeks ago. We set on 'em and I says, "Billy, you do the lights, OK? Set so you can reach 'em. Wait till I say though, OK?" He scooted up on the top bale close to the switch. We waited only five, ten minutes, I was just startin' to daydream when I heard the gnawin', that unmistakable gnawin', uhn ah uhn ah uhn ah, don't let up neither, 'cause they mean business.

I whisper, "Billy, that's it. Hear? Over there, hear?" I stood up, got the potato hook, both hands.

"Now keep your eyes peeled case he runs off." There was no change in the gnawin' with my whisperin'. "OK, Billy, now."

Sure enough, there he was, settin' right on one of the last of the wooden stanchions. He lifted his head just as slow and cocky, sauntered down the aisle just as slow till I start to come up behind him, he starts then to waddle like a old fat lady hurryin'. I got him right back of the neck with the potato hook. He starts shakin' his head mad and I says, "Oh Billy, oh Billy," and then, "Damn!" 'cause I lost him till I come down again right 'hind his neck and I knowed then I had to hold it real tight, the prongs, they don't even come close to his hide.

Problem was, I was behind him and I had to git him facin'
me so I could git his nose. I tried to twist him around but I
couldn't. I says, "Kruppy Cole, where are you, damnit!" Then
I let him go so as I could run around front of him and git him
again head on. "Thank God, Billy," I says, "this is one hell
of a slow animal." Then it come to me I had to do it, I had
him smack front of me. Inside I shout, "Here goes!" and I
flipped it, come down on the end of his face with the back of
the hook. Whack! But it wasn't hard enough or right 'cause
he looked up soon as I started to do it and I seen his eyes
and I stopped a little and he curled his nose in soon as the
hook raise off him. I did it again and again and again, I was
whackin' whatever I could reach, tryin' for his nose, he
was buryin' that damn nose, and each time I come down it
was soft, he was soft, the porcupine was soft, and the back
of the hook was hard and comin' down on soft and I was
sayin', "Oh Billy, oh Billy, oh Billy," the whole time till he
wasn't movin' no more, and I straightened up and he moved
and I whacked him one more time. I was shakin', I says,
"Goddamnit, would you just die?" but he wouldn't, he kept
tryin' to move after a minute or so layin' still and I had to
whack him again. Finally, I stood over him seemed a whole
two minutes, my potato hook ready, but he didn't move no
more and I gone over to where Billy was standin' 'bout ten
feet back and I says, "Let's set down, I gotta set down. We'll
keep the lights on awhile."

Billy, he put his hand on my knee like a adult and he says,
"You had to, right? Kill him, right?"

I nodded. I started to say, "But it ain't nice." I couldn't say
nothin' though. *You gotta stop shakin', Margaret. You just
gotta stop and git on with it.*

I closed my eyes. *Where's the bull when I need him? Maybe
he don't like this work neither.* I whisper to Billy, "Turn 'em
off." I heard the flick and the white under my eyelids turned

black and I set there tryin' to git used to the black. We both heard it.

"Damnit!" I whisper sharp. "Can't they wait a respectful time 'fore they walk right up to git killed?"

"Now," I says and Billy hit the switch and I seen it after a few seconds, it got farther away than the first one, though this time I knowed to git it head on first thing, I says to it, I says, "Don't you dare look at me," and it didn't, and it only took 'bout five hits 'fore it lay still.

I didn't see no more of their eyes and I got better and better, till it was almost dawn and we hear number fourteen. It come a job by this time, a dirty job but I was almost enjoyin' it, that I was doin' it right, so a few times it'd take only two hits, and I kept every one from lookin' up at me. But the last one, he tricked me.

I come down with the back end of the hook, it was the second blow, and I knew it was gonna do it and soon as it hit, I give out, inside I give out, like I was all finished and I let down. Soon as I did, just before he gone still, it was only a split second, he look up at me, the porcupine, and that look shot through a split-second hole I was too tired to guard, I seen into his eyes and I gone black—I guess Billy was callin' me a long time.

It was all dark, darker'n night, and I wasn't walkin', I was movin' though 'cause there was a bright light at one end, like I was in a culvert underground, floatin' toward the openin' at the end but it was tiny, the openin', seemed even a kid couldn't fit. I was hearin' my name over and over but it seem so far off and like it wasn't my name, it was only familiar kinda. Then it come. "MOMMY!" Stopped me dead, it was from behind me, the sound was comin' from behind me, I was scareder'n I'd ever been 'cause I knew I had to turn around and go back. I kept sayin', "Turn. Turn, now. Turn, now." Finally, I did, I turned even though I was movin' back into the dark, into the ground, and I thought, *I'm gonna suffocate*. But I didn't, I came to, I was on the floor and Billy was right over my face and he looked full of nothin' but terror, and his tears was hittin' me, my face, it was all wet, and I says, "Billy, oh my God, Billy," and I grabbed him and I hug him so hard I think he's gonna burst. He was stiff as a board and hot, too, and I was huggin' the stiffness right outa him but not the heat.

20

The Killing

I OPEN MY EYES and there's Doro, settin' on the end of the bed, starin' off. It was two-thirty in the afternoon, Billy and me gone to bed after breakfast. I didn't tell nothin' to Tappen 'cept that I got fourteen of 'em, but Doro I told the whole thing to. I look over to Billy. He's sound asleep on his back, how he does — his arms spread out like he's floatin', he's throwed off every cover and sheet ever land on him.

I git up on one elbow, cock myself toward Doro. "You know," I says, and she turn toward me. "It was a good thing, I'm lucky Billy was there."

"I'll help you tonight, Margaret," she says, only her face was turned.

I nodded. I had a flash again of that tiny openin' at the end of the culvert, that light, and everything suddenly seem so dim, dark compared to That, daylight was nothin' compared to That.

"I don't think I woulda died or nothin' but I got . . . I got confused, I was headin' the wrong way, I was headin' toward the light, I was all . . . confused."

"You never killed anything before, did you?" she said.

"Nope," I said. "I never did." I kinda smiled at myself. Here I was yesterday, big hero, tryin' to protect *her*.

"It's not gonna happen again, is it, Margaret?" she said.

"Nope," I says. "It ain't. It can't. The horse barn, we should do the horse barn tonight."

I remembered the cow barn! "Shit!" I yelled and throwed the covers back. "What?" I heard Doro say. "Where the hell you goin'?" But I had already grabbed my jeans and my jacket, I was almost to the stairs. I stuck my legs into my pants by the kitchen door and shoved my feet into the fronts of my sneakers and run out, zippin' my pants up on the way and tryin' to git my heels in without stoppin', I had my coat in my teeth, I checked my pockets, yup, there was my gloves. I looked back toward the house. Doro wasn't followin', thank God.

Tappen was finally movin' the hay we sat on into one of his box stalls he don't use. "Well, why are you so wide-eyed and breathless?" he said, and straightened up toward me. He got both strings of a bale in his one hand, he was about to pick up another, then he stopped, looked at me.

"Where are all the porcupines, Tappen?" I says.

"In back," he said. "Now hold up," he said and he set the bale down. "Settle down a minute. They ain't burned or nothin'. They woulda been, I got the gasoline right over there ready to soak 'em, but Eudora, she come out here like she was savin' the world and she says I gotta wait, said Margaret might wanna do sump'n with 'em. Now you gonna have a simple funeral or you want a full-blown procession?"

I took a deep breath. "Thanks, Tappen," I says and headed for the door out to the pasture.

"By the manure spreader," he yelled after me, probably shakin' his head, thinkin', "Them girls."

They was all in a heap, you couldn't see none of their heads, just a bunch of thick coats, the hair stickin' straight up, not shinin' a bit in the full sun, and the quills bunched together pretty thick on their backs and tails. They looked ugly. I put on my gloves and sorted through 'em fast, though even with my gloves the quills kept stickin'. I was sortin' through, lookin' at their faces, till finally it come to me. *You ain't gonna find him, Margaret.*

Then I thought, *Shit, you killed 'em all, it wasn't just the last one done it, it was each one of 'em, it was the job, it was all of 'em pilin' into a job, into a rhythm, it was the rhythm done it.*

I hurried quick 'cause I didn't want Doro to come out, see me, I pulled a quill from each one of 'em. I made sure I didn't miss none of 'em. I stood up, put my hand that was holdin' 'em in my coat pocket and just in time, I seen Doro come out from the cow barn.

She come over, she says, "You wanna bury 'em?"

"Nope," I says, still holdin' fast to them quills. "I ain't a ceremony person like you. Tappen, he can burn 'em, I don't care."

Even though Billy slept till three, at eight-thirty I says, "OK, Billy, time to brush your teeth." I never let him go to bed without brushin' his teeth, nope, he ain't gonna have false teeth or a black mouth neither, not if I can help it. We git into bed and he starts talkin' gibberish. We just started doin' it 'bout a week ago, it ain't easy to keep up a flow like you're really talkin' and not repeat the same sounds over and over. He started askin' questions, and I was answerin', then we was yellin', makin' all sorts of faces and hand movements like we was Italian or colored and it almost seem after a while we knew what we was sayin' 'cause the make-up words, they sort of change dependin' on how you're feelin', or pretendin' you're feelin'. Like first we was soundin' Chinese or sump'n, Japanese, and then it turn into sort of a Spanish, then we was stuck on *k*'s for a while, everything had a *k* in it. Every time we switched — we didn't plan to switch or nothin', it just kinda grows that way — it seem a different part of you come out.

Finally, Billy settle down into a soft, almost whisper gibberish and then I lean over his face and I says, whisperin', too, "You can stay in tonight if you want to, you know."

He look up at me and nodded, closed his eyes, noddin'.

I watched him while he was fallin' into sleep. 'Fore supper, how he follow me upstairs with a grin on his face, boy! after I says into his ear, I says, "I got a present for you, come on," and I grabbed my coat. I closed the door to our room and took the quills outa the pocket and I says, "There's one from every one of 'em." He took 'em from me, his little fingers circlin' 'round the bunch so careful, he squat down on the floor then and lean over 'em lookin' like he was studyin' every inch of 'em. They was cream-colored and they shined so under the light, they was beautiful, and the bit of black on 'em, you could see into it, like a jewel, like that black jewel I can't think the name of, but it sound like a animal or sump'n. Billy looked at 'em and then he look back at me and then he looked at 'em again and then he look back at me. Then he started pokin' the back of his finger with one of 'em. I watched him and I seen he ain't stoppin', he pushed straight on in till I see a little bead of blood come out and I says, "Billy!" and he flinched like I just burst in. I says, "I got a old sock you can keep 'em in, Billy." And I pulled it out from my top drawer. "Now this is our secret, hear?" I said. "Don't you let no one know I give you 'em. This is our secret." We hid 'em then, and ain't a soul ever gonna know where either, on my account.

Billy was asleep. *Tonight, Billy, I'm gonna learn to kill. Maybe someday I can teach you, maybe.*

But there wasn't nothin' to learn, or nothin' to learn that someone can teach you, it just happened. It was my sixth one. Doro and me was takin' turns. Doro wasn't that good with the

Cole style at first though I told her to make sure she gits the porcupine head on first thing. She said after her first one, "A gun is easier," but I said, "I hate the sound," so we did it Kruppy's way.

It musta been three, four o'clock and he give me his eyes like a few of 'em had done already and I didn't stiffen up 'gainst 'em like I done before, I didn't feel all guarded, tryin' to stare him out. 'Stead, I look into them eyes and I feel sump'n shoot outa mine, it was almost, almost *love*, it was like love but you coulda touched it and it shoot from my eyes into his, it was just as I was swingin' the handle, just before he got the whack, that love, it seem to push him, send him off and he was dead in one blow and Doro, she come up behind me. "Holy," she says. "One hit." And I said, "I done it, Doro, I done it and I didn't even try," and I sat down.

It was that time right 'fore dawn when it ain't light yet but the dark don't seem as dark no more. We sat there and waited one more hour, and not one more porcupine came. We had gotten eleven.

Finally, the windows started to turn gray and Doro says to me, "Margaret, what do you . . . what are you . . . what do you think we should do about Beulah?"

I stiffen inside. "Shit," I says, and I know she thinks I'm sayin' 'shit' about Beulah but I ain't, I'm sayin' it about Doro. I don't say nothin' more. She was waitin' and waitin' but she don't have that suckin' ability Beulah has, that waitin' that seem to pull things right outa you no matter and though I knowed it wasn't fair, I didn't say nothin' more.

Finally, she says, "Well?"

I git up and grab the potato hook and start to walk toward the front door. Tappen just limed the concrete yesterday, makes the floor look all shiny in the new light. Doro followed me out. She don't try to catch up to me though. She usually walks faster'n me, but she was walkin' just my pace. I lean the potato hook up against the sidin', open the kitchen door, and turn 'round and wait for her.

"I ain't gonna do nothin', is what I'm tellin you, Doro."

I look at her square in the eyes and shake my head and I seen she was pleadin' and then I seen she was scared, more'n scared, she was like a kid full of terror. I keep starin', I don't stop, and I keep shakin' my head, I ain't lettin' her pass, I stand there shakin' my head, pinnin' her with my eyes till I seen the terror back off, and she starts noddin' her head, noddin' her head, and she squeeze her eyes closed and I says, "Yup," and we both walk into the kitchen together.

21

Grace

I GUESS IT DIDN'T happen that fast, Beulah gittin' sick again.
We wasn't ready for it, that's all. Tappen, he gone on, looked
no different to an outsider, but to us, we knew, forty-six years
they was married. Beulah was seventeen, Tappen was nine-
teen. "He was just a boy then, really," Beulah'd said, "but he
seemed a man to me, yup, he was a man enough to me and
that's all it took for me to marry him. Things was different
then."

I was settin' on the front of the chair Tappen uses as a closet,
a week's worth of work pants and the coveralls we only wash
once a month he got draped over the back. I pulled the chair
up side of her bed, they got twin beds, hers is closest to the
door. I drink down half my coffee so it don't spill and lean
onto the bed, close in to her, she was talkin' real low.

I been up here with her after breakfast 'bout half an hour,
an hour every day — well, just the last two weeks, she ain't
gotten up since her stools started bleedin' so bad. I brought a
plant stand up from the porch to put the basin on she vomits

into 'cause her bedside table is chocked so full the lamp is pushed all the way to the edge. There's the box of Kleenex and about ten bunched-up ones I try to keep thrown but Beulah only lets 'em go if there ain't a square inch left to 'em. Then she got her aspirin she don't use no more and the pills the doctor give her stuck 'hind the lamp which is the shape of a fancy lady in a green evenin' gown which is swirlin' into her arms which are swirlin', too, over her head into the light. The pills are in two boxes, together they're almost the size of a shoe box, filled all with separate packages, you gotta poke the pills out the foil in the back, they're what you call samples, Beulah didn't pay nothin' for 'em. She got her stack of peppermints, big chocolate ones, though they ain't goin' quick, the top one wrapped back up is only 'bout half done and that took her three days. She only puts a tiny bit into her mouth each time to git rid of the sour taste, she don't really swallow it since she ain't been keepin' nothin' down.

She got a bell, too, a old cow bell every kid been in the house has had by 'em whenever they was sick, you can hear it even from the cellar. Beulah rings it when she needs the bedpan, and though she ain't usin' it much the last couple of days, I still been stayin' pretty close to the house. Only when Laureen comes, 'bout maybe every other day for a few hours she ain't workin', when she comes I go shoppin' or I get Ida over with, so Tappen don't have to come in till supper. Closest to Beulah, even closer than the bell, is the bunch of the first dandelions come up Debbie and Billy brung her, they've dried more'n wilted and still look kinda pretty in the jelly jar.

Beulah told me about Jimmy Marr and his sister Karen, she whispered just sayin' their names. She never even mentioned 'em before. She was babysittin' for 'em, Laureen was about six, in school already, and the ma, she never come back, and they was sunburned so bad when she dropped 'em off, Beulah said, the top of their heads and everything, the ma had left 'em both out in the sun all day in the playpen, not even a shirt on, and Jimmy only twelve weeks old. Karen, she was three. "You couldn't even hold 'em that first night, they was cryin' so to touch 'em," Beulah said. Four years she had 'em, and those times Tappen wasn't doin' so well and she had to go out to keep 'em, she cleaned with Iola Clark then, they had twenty-two houses 'tween 'em. "Oh, I loved those kids so," she says, and her eyes water up and she starts blinkin' so she don't let nothin' drip. Four years and then the mother come back, says she wants to git to know 'em, take 'em out for ice cream down at what used to be Ellie's, and the ma, she took 'em clear to Illinois, and then Beulah puts in after, after she makes sure she ain't gonna cry, she says, "Karen, she had it the worse."

There was a patter on the stairs we knowed was Debbie, how she scampers up feet and hands both, and she come burstin' in—Laureen musta just dropped her off, she works all through the weekend—she comes runnin' in and jumps on Beulah's bed, and though she don't seem careful she is, 'cause she jumps right past the plant stand but she don't touch it, she's yellin', "Grandma, Grandma," knowin' her grandma don't have a "no" in her body.

Her body that's bloatin' up every day more and more like a balloon, swellin' up ever since her bowels stopped movin' a week ago and she started throwin' first food back up, even plain food like noodles and rice, not even any butter on 'em, then tea, now sometimes even water. She started turnin' yellow then, too, deeper every day, and I don't mean what Doro sees underneath. This was her skin, yesterday she was almost bright, even Tappen seen it clear as day.

I says, "Beulah, it ain't the bull, is it?" and she looks at me, shakes her head. She got one arm 'round Debbie's waist. Debbie's standin' right 'side all the pillows stacked up under Beulah, shiftin' her feet like a filly, she don't seem to mind the smell, got both her arms 'round her grandma's neck. The smell come from Beulah's belchin' though it seem pretty calm today. Beulah shakes her head. "Nope," she says. "It ain't. I'm just fillin' up, Margaret, with the wrong stuff," and she touch the top of my hand.

I says, "You glad you went to Brigham?" I never asked her and it's been two weeks now. The bull or the doctor, neither of us brung 'em up.

"Oh," she says, "he's a nice man. He's a nice man and I says straight to him as I walk in, I says, 'I know it's cancer, Doctor, and you probably thinkin' I'm gonna tell you it's the bull.' He sat right down front of me in that chair of his. I tell you, Margaret, he seein' me even alive after how bad I was, I coulda told him it's a frog in there and he'd've believed me. I says to him, 'I know it's cancer and I know it's stupid for me to be here 'cause I ain't goin' to no hospital, I ain't havin' no operation, I got myself a big hole that's fillin' up and when it's all filled up I'm gonna die in peace.' I says that to him and he sets there just starin' at me till he says, 'You're smarter'n all of us, probably.'

"He give me these samples outa his drawer, they're for the pain, and I got out to Mrs. Brigham, she's the secretary, he didn't charge me nothin'."

That was the first time I heard the word "cancer" in that house in about six months, like it wasn't just a word no more but a thing, a piece of furniture no one could touch or come near, and it was settin' in the middle of every room and we was all walkin' big circles 'round it.

Every day Beulah ask me 'bout Billy if he ain't with me, if he's gone off to watch Doro train the horses in the small corral. I've told her 'bout when he tried to eat a spit bug and how he feeds the dogs on the sly so they follow him around now like a magnet. After Debbie run off to the horse barn, too, I says to Beulah, I says, "Guess what Billy come out with yesterday, Beulah. He says to me—he's poopin', and you know he hates bein' alone in there, and it takes him a full ten minutes, so he decides he's gonna start a actual conversation keep me hooked—he says to me, 'Margaret'—he calls me Ma, too, but that's mostly nighttime—'Margaret, girls don't pee like people do.' And I tease him, I says, course after I inform him that we girls are people, too, I says, 'So you got a regular peein' machine, huh?' And he give me a look, he says, 'Margaret,' like I am du-umb, 'it ain't a 'chine, Margaret, it's just a plain penis.' "

Beulah, she chuckles and she come up close, she says, "Now you remind him of that when he's eighteen, hear?"

It come up then, a bunch of vomit looks like spit, and I almost gag though I'm usually real good with that kind of stuff. Even in those tests we took in high school, I'm the basic nursin' personality, they says. And they're right 'cause it takes a lot make me gag. Beulah, she seen my face and she says, "Hang on there, Margaret," as she put the basin back on the stand, and I smile and think, *Am I gonna miss you.*

I says, "Can you git down some macaroni and cheese? It's Billy's favorite."

She said, "You can bring a little up," though we both knowed she wasn't gonna eat it, it was a thing we kept up, she knew I had to do it.

I usually told her everything I was gonna make for supper but I didn't tell her I bought mashed potato buds 'cause the potatoes was all gone—well, there was a few left but they was so sprouted and soft as marshmallows, too. Beulah woulda dropped through the bed if I told her I got boxed potatoes, even in the store I practically stuffed the box in the cashier's nose, 'cause I felt I was stealin' sump'n just buyin' 'em, till I says to myself, "Margaret, Beulah ain't gonna cook again so you do what you want, there's no sin to boxed potatoes."

"You're doin' good, Maggie," she says lookin' straight ahead. "Real good."

I swallowed. She never called me that before, no one

has, though outa her mouth it was me, all right, Maggie. It was private, too, just 'tween her and me. I knew then what Doro felt when Beulah called her "Dorrie" that first day she come. How she named Bubby, too. I wanna stroke her hair, or comb it, but I don't, I git up. I walk over to git the basin.

"You send Billy up here, you hear?"

"OK," I says and smile. She musta known I didn't let him come up yesterday 'cept to kiss her good night 'cause he ain't as gentle as Debbie, jumps right on top of her. She wouldn't flinch, course, let him know she's hurtin'. No, she gotta act like she's a little boy, too, doublin' up her fists front of her face, pretendin' she's gonna punch, she gits him all jumpy and I git worried.

She says to me when I come back in with the empty basin, she says, "Margaret, Doro's uhm . . ."

"She'll come up," I says. "She's just been so busy and all, you know she's been right 'side helpin' Tappen and trainin' five horses, too. Some guy called up yesterday, I says to him without even tellin' her, I says, 'She's all filled up till August.' She woulda killed me if she knowed, but . . ."

Beulah just nodded. I left. *Shit. I run my mouth off when I don't say the truth.* It ain't I'm lyin', it's I ain't sayin' IT, ain't sayin' to Beulah that Doro ain't come up here in four days 'cause she can't bear seein' you die and her doin' nothin' 'bout it. Tappen, he's sinkin', but Doro, she don't know how to be still and just sink, her hands always gotta be doin' sump'n. I bet there ain't a minute goes by—her canterin' 'round on those horses, figure eights and everything—she ain't tryin' to figure some way she can wake up outa this dream and change it so Beulah don't die. Like Billy she is, like Billy when he run up 'gainst a "no!"

None of us ever said straight out, "Beulah's gonna die," none of us. I done sump'n close to it though, right over the macaroni and cheese. I says grace. Tappen look up and then look right down again on his plate, ain't no one ever said grace 'cept Beulah and so we ain't heard it at supper in over a month. Billy, Debbie, they had their forks raised midair, stopped right in midair.

"Bless this food, dear Lord," I says. Doro, she stares down at her hands folded on her lap, the fingers is hooked but the rest is open so as she can see her palms and her wrists, too, she's starin' at her palms.

> "Bless this food, dear Lord.
> And may we give Thee thanks
> For the fellowship of our table
> And for the bounty here before us.
> May we use it to Thy glory. Amen."

The whole goddamn dinner goin' by and ain't anyone sayin' nothin'. Finally, I blurt out, "Well, someone's gotta say it, grace. Beulah can't, someone's gotta start sayin' it."

Tappen, Doro, they ain't chewin'. They ain't lookin' up neither. I says more, I says, "She's gonna die, ain't anybody gonna say it? Straight out? Ain't anybody else gonna say it? She's gonna die."

Doro look quick at Billy, then Debbie, like I'm talkin' dirty.

"You think they don't know it? They're up there every day, they're up there every hour. You think they don't know it? Huh? Huh?

"And there ain't nothin' we can do 'cept . . . 'cept eat our macaroni and cheese, eat the macaroni and cheese. You hear me, Doro? Eat it, hear? Ain't nothin' we can do but eat the food 'cause this here food . . . just . . . you better just eat it . . ." I was almost cryin' though I managed to git out "I'm sorry" to Tappen. He never looked up. He was lookin' straight, not at his plate but a little front of it, and eatin', he was scoopin' up the macaroni, starin' fixed half a foot front of his plate, his plate emptyin' and he wasn't even lookin'.

Doro, she was lookin' down steady onto her plate, eatin'. The kids was eatin'. No one asked for more, but no one stopped neither. There wasn't even a spot of orange left on the plates, not even the kids' plates, every plate looked licked clean.

22

Hole

DORO, A FEW NIGHTS LATER, she was smokin' a cigarette out in the horse barn, settin' right on the cement under the saddles in the tack room. I says, "Eudora!"

She held her cigarette up front of her face, looked at it, then at me and Billy. "I used to smoke a lot when I was a kid." she said. "Always alone though, I always smoked alone, never with anybody. I haven't in . . . a long time, a lo-ong time." She took another drag.

"Billy," I says, "don't you ever smoke." And we set down beside her, though I had to shove over a bag of salt blocks and a bag of empty feed bags, too, so we had room. I come out to tell her Beulah's been in a coma since, well, at least supper, maybe longer, since Tappen left her 'bout half an hour 'fore we ate and gone up again after I done the dishes. He shook her to see if she'd wake up — he's done that a few times till she moves or sump'n 'cause the doctor told him she might go into a coma — he shook her and tapped her face, she didn't twitch or nothin' and then he lifted up her eyelid, and her pupil, it was wide open.

I just set there up 'gainst the tack room wall, not sayin' nothin'. Billy, too, 'side me, just set there. The wall's rough pine, same as Doro used for the stalls. She made all them box stalls, five of 'em. There was just standin' stalls in here 'fore, but she wouldn't keep a horse tied all day, Tappen said. No sirree, not Doro. Sixteen years old she got her first horse, she learned how to hammer a nail same week. I waited through her whole cigarette, quiet, like we was huddlin' 'round a fire.

"Tappen gone up to Beulah," I says finally. "She ain't . . . awake, she ain't breathin' regular neither. He tried to git hold of Laureen but she ain't at work."

Doro nodded, took a long drag. The horses was stampin' a little in their stalls, snortin', too. She had three of the horses in, two out. Their noises, they was warm. I didn't want 'em to quiet, I didn't want to leave, go back to the house.

"You know, Margaret, I went up there today," Doro said.

I turned and looked at her. Billy, he was nuzzlin' his head like a dog 'tween my belly and my thigh so he could lay his head on my lap. I straightened my legs, put my arm down 'cross his shoulder.

"I can't see anymore," Doro says. "I can't see, ever since the porcupines. I look at Beulah, I can't see in, I can't tell."

"It's OK, Doro," I says. "It don't matter, it's OK."

She stamped out her cigarette on the cement beside her and picked up the pack, they was Camels, she got another one out. I says, "You gonna smoke the whole pack in one night?" And she nodded, says, "Yup."

She smiled while she took a puff, and she says, "There was this guy named Eddie, at Kaatersville, I always called him just Ed, he was two grades ahead of me. I was only fifteen but I wanted, well, I had had"—she was smilin', boy, like she was still fifteen—"I had come already, ridin' a horse." She started laughin', I was gigglin'. "It was durin' a lesson, too," she said. "Jerry Hendrickson, she was gittin' me to push with my seat.

Ya see, you gotta push with your butt forward just like you're fuckin'," and she looked down toward Billy to see if his eyes was closed, he was breathin' pretty steady. "You gotta do it every time the horse moves his back end forward and in a trot, that's quite a rhythm, and I felt it comin'. I didn't know what it was, really, though it was definitely comin', and we were supposed to be doin' a perfect circle, I mean per-fect, the arc, and Jerry's shoutin', 'Push push push push,' and I'm doin' it and doin' it right, and doin' it right is makin' it come closer, and as soon as I miss or stop, Jerry yells, 'No, no,' 'cause she's lookin' at the horse's back end to see the effect I'm havin'. All of a sudden I fall right forward onto my horse's neck, hidin' my face, and my horse, Splash was her name, goes all the hell out the circle and off, she stops under this apple tree we'd stay under to wait for our turn on the jumps. Jerry, she looked at me so confused as I walked Splash back toward her all flushed and then she broke out into a smile. I knew she knew, and she nods and says, 'Start again,' like nothin' ever happened.

"But ever since, I looked at this guy Ed different, and you know why?" She looked straight at me, smilin'. "You know why? Two reasons," she says. "His hips and his forearms," she says, and I cracked up.

"You was *fifteen?*" I says and she nodded. I says, "Boy, was I slow."

"He had these small hips," she said and raised her hands to show me just how small, "but mostly, Margaret, mostly it was his, his forearms, they were so . . . veiny . . . He seemed so . . . so old. See, he helped his dad weekends, his dad was a contractor. Ed was seventeen, he had an old car he drove around but it wasn't souped up loud like the rest of the guys' cars. It was just old, beat up, a Mustang or somethin'. I couldn't stop lookin' at him durin' lunch, and in the hall, too, that was the only time I got to see him, so I gave him a note. It said, I remember this so clear, I remember writin' it, it said, 'I've never done it before and I want to with you.' I gave it to him right in the hall while he was throwin' books into his locker. At lunch the next day, he gives me a note back and stands right there while I open it and it says, 'Really?' and I look at him and I nod, and he says, 'Come on,' and I follow him out the back door. That was practically under Mr. Nelson's window. I followed him right out in broad daylight and we get in his car and I say, 'I know a good place.' We didn't say one word the whole time drivin', not one. Not even when we got out of the car on top of Devil's Ridge and he followed me to that place where there was a break from the hardhack and thorn apples. I said then, 'We better stop here.'

"I hadn't even kissed a man yet and it took a while till I was kissin' him back, but soon as I did, he had my shirt off. It was late September, it was pretty cold, we were on top of our clothes, but I was there, Margaret, on my back and my legs wide open and he couldn't get in, it was that damn hymen, I found out later, blockin' him. He pushed and pushed, I was a bit in a daze, I didn't know if this was IT or not until finally, he said, 'You certainly *are* a virgin, aren't you?' and he pulled away and laid his head down on my belly.

"We tried two more times and then he made it in, but by that time I was pretty numb and I didn't know exactly when it had changed, when he was actually in, and all I remember is he stopped movin' and then he said, pretty softly, 'Was it OK for you?' And I thought, 'Oh my God, that was it. I missed it.' I kept him on top of me a long time after that just layin' there, and he missed a study hall and I missed social studies and Mr. Nelson called up Tappen and he came and talked to me out in the barn, he said, 'So you're in heat, huh?' But he promised he wouldn't tell Beulah and he never did. It was our secret." She stamped out her cigarette right by the other though it wasn't half done.

I was just settin' there lookin' at her. "Shit," Doro said. "We better go in, don't ya think?"

I picked Billy up onto my shoulder 'fore I got up. Thirty-four pounds, Beulah was happy of that, boy.

Doro was closin' up the barn lights and I stood there on the ramp she built and the stars, they was so clear, there was the Big Dipper and the W and a few stars of the Little Dipper, too.

I heard her behind me slidin' the door open even wider for the night and I said, "Doro, their light's on."

"Yeah," she said, and we started walkin' toward the house, Doro first and me with Billy all limp behind, down the path mostly Doro made.

The light was off again by the time we got upstairs. Doro come into my room and we both laid down right on the spread, I was by the wall, I set Billy 'tween us, gave him the pillow. We kept the light on. We was on our backs, had our hands 'hind our heads like they was pillows, we was waitin'.

Doro heard Tappen first, she heard him git outa bed. He walked down the hall and stalled by our door but then kept on goin' down the stairs to the phone. We knew he got hold of Laureen 'cause we could hear him talkin' though we couldn't make out the words. We heard him walk back up the stairs, we both sat up and I slid over, around Billy, we both sat on the side of the bed facin' the door.

Tappen stopped, opened the door, and stood there in the doorway. "You better come in," he said.

Doro was first up. We walked down the hall followin' Tappen. I'd never been in their room with *both* of 'em. Their room had always been so private, even visitin' just Beulah and seein' Tappen's things around, it took me a while not to feel like a peepin' Tom. Tappen opened the door and Doro walked in, then me, then Tappen closed the door 'hind us.

Me and Doro walked around Beulah's bed and sat on Tappen's. He didn't have no pillow. The light on the bedside table was on, the fancy lady swirlin' her way into the light. Beulah was almost upright, propped up with three pillows. She looked just asleep but real still. She was breathin' fast, then it slowed to normal, then it turned on fast again.

I seen the book on the table, the little blue book of sonnets Doro's ma wrote. It was on its side by the peppermints, leanin' up against the jelly jar of dried-up dandelions. Doro must've just give it to her today when she snuck up to see Beulah alone after almost a week of stayin' away.

I'm real, real tired, I thought. I wanted to curl up right next to Beulah like Debbie or Billy always done, curl right up next to her and just 'fore I fall asleep feel her arm come around me so I wouldn't fall off the edge.

Her hand moved a little, waved a little to the side like she was paddlin' herself in water, like her hand was a fin. Tappen stood up.

"Clay," I thought she said, barely, I coulda sworn. "Clay."

Doro's body stiffened next to me. Clay Tappen, her husband. He set down on the bed with her but she didn't wake up.

I git up, I ain't thinkin', I move to the other side of her bed, other side from Tappen closest to the door, I set down, there ain't much room side of her legs. Beulah's head is all the way thrown back on the pillow, she's breathin' heavy, she got her mouth open, breathin' fast, slow, when she breathe out it gurgled a little, like she was breathin' through water. *I wanna see her eyes. I gotta see her eyes.* I lean right to her, touch her forehead. She don't move. She don't even twitch. I pull her skin on her forehead up, away from her eyes.

"Open 'em, Beulah, open your eyes," I says. "I wanna see your eyes. Come on, Beulah, open 'em up now."

I opened her eyes with my fingers, held 'em open. The pupils was huge.

"Beulah, Beulah, look at me, Beulah."

Doro was up. "Margaret, don't, come on, don't." But I waved her off, and she sat right down again.

"Look at me, Beulah." I had her eyes pointin' straight at me. "Look at me, Beulah." I wanted to dive, I was tilted forward, another inch I coulda fallen in, I coulda dove into 'em. That voice come though, kept me upright, kept me from takin' off with her, that cold voice bottom of my butt keepin' my back straight, keepin' me from that . . . Beulah's . . . pond water it is, like warm pond water I coulda bathed in for another minute, I coulda been with her another minute, but that cold voice come, sayin', "No! Don't!"

I didn't lean forward, I didn't back up, I stood there holdin' her eyelids open with my fingers and Tappen, I felt his shoulder right there side of me. "She could go on another week like this, you know," I says. "We can't let her go on like this, we gotta let her go."

I sent it, I sent everything I could, outa my eyes and into them eyes that didn't seem eyes no more, seem just pits, just a hole, and way in there, way deep in was Beulah, waitin'. I gave her every last ounce of push I had. I had to reach her, I had to git it to her, what I had that could help her move, git through. I sent her only one shot and then I collapsed, right on her belly, I heard Doro sink down onto the floor from Tappen's bed, Tappen didn't let nothin' out, I smelled his work pants, my face was right 'gainst his work pants, they was clean but they still had a grease smell, grease and washin' detergent, he didn't let nothin' out.

I laid on her belly and I felt it, without even lookin', it mighta been ten minutes, half hour, I don't know. She left. I felt it. I squeezed my eyes, squeezed 'em tight shut. She left. I didn't let go, I couldn't let go, not yet. I stayed there on her belly. Tappen whispered, "Oh God, no." He had her whole arm.

It took Tappen the longest to leave her. You could tell with each of us when we stopped lookin' for her, with me I was holdin' her belly till I felt it come up through her nightgown, the cold, and like metal, too, not even like wood, the cold was like metal and it come right through her nightgown and I lifted myself up, though I kept lookin' for her. Till I says almost out loud, "She ain't there," and I got up off the bed, and Doro, she started to git up, too, she was right side of Tappen's legs, right on his calves, she was on the floor leanin' onto his calves. She got up but like she was lost, like she had to git on a train but she was a little girl, needed a conductor take her hand.

"Tappen," I said. "Tappen, you wanna stay?" He didn't say nothin'. He was hung on to her arm, her bicep, it was soakin' wet, he didn't make no noise but her nightgown was soakin' wet and he hung on to it like it was holdin' him to shore.

Doro and me gone out together, left him in there alone with her. Laureen come in through the kitchen then, it was 2:45, end of her shift. Though we didn't say nothin', she seen by our faces that she didn't make it, she run past us, up the stairs.

It was Doro called the doctor though I said, "Wait till mornin', he can't do nothin' anyway." Dr. Brigham told us to call Bunner. But we didn't call him till dawn when Tappen come down.

I handed Tappen a cup of coffee and he drunk it standin' up. His face had a red blotch on it. From her arm, her stiff shoulder up against his cheek. Doro was at the counter fixin' toast. "Want some?" she says to Tappen, and he just nodded.

Bunner come with one of his workers, it was before eight, and he's got what he calls a body bag and I gone into the room again and I see her and I forget everything and I wanna hold her again like she's in there, or comb her hair, but she ain't, and I says, "Oh my God," like it just come to me she was dead.

I set down on her bed after they got her out, I didn't wanna see any more of the bag, them carryin' her down the stairs. I set down on her bed.

"I wanna talk to you," I says. Then I says, "Stop, Margaret, stop. Don't you send a word."

It was like stoppin' a flood. I wanted to tell her 'bout supper and cleanin' Tappen's shirts and Billy and how we can't plant beans yet 'cause it's gone cold again. I stopped every word 'cept one. "The hole, go toward the hole."

It's so little. And I think of that big plastic bag with the zipper and how when they lifted it off the bed it was stiff and I think of that light, that long, narrow tunnel with that tiny, brighter'n bright hole. Billy, he comes in, his fist in his eyes, rubs up 'gainst my thigh and I says, "She done it, Billy, she's made it, all the way through, she ain't gonna stop now, Billy, not for no one."

23

Brand

Jo. Dressed in pants and a man's shirt, a white shirt, wrinkled up and one collar button undone. I seen 'cause I watched her steady all through the receivin' line at the funeral, seen her shake Doro's hand, stare right into Doro's eyes, she didn't flinch. Yup, everything comes from luck and you can't worry if it's bad or good 'cause you can't tell which is which anyway.

I sat on the bottom rail, my head squinched under the top, watchin' Billy face one of Tappen's cows movin' toward him, her head movin' side to side, like them dice swingin' off Jo's mirror side to side whenever that car goes, side to side, then comin' still. She's starin' at him, just as still, head on. "Go on, Billy honey, go on through now, Billy. Now."

Daddy, he dropped us one at a time into Walzak's pond, Sharon, Billy, and me, we was learnin' how to swim. Illegal, 'cause it wasn't our pond. Daddy dropped me and I thought I was dyin' and then I come up, I was all curled but I felt it. I was bein' raised up just 'fore he grabbed me, I was cryin' hard but I still heard him say, "See, it can carry you, don't fight it,

*it'll carry you." I didn't believe him then, I was cryin' too hard
but it turned out true, another two, three times and it was
true.*

"Billy Hart, you come on back now, come on."

Little wave run through his shoulders.

I says sharp, "Don't you ever go in without me, without me
right 'side you, hear? I'll tan your hide.

"I got more to teach you 'bout it, hear? You hear?" He
nods.

"It's dangerous, understand?" He keeps noddin'.

"As dangerous as a pond." He's noddin' away.

"OK," I says. "Don't shake your head off."

He look up at me and a shiver run through me, I done it
now, I give it to him, the brand. Billy and me now, we're like
twins, twin fists.

Doro, she gone on a rampage. Said she smelled death, smelled
it from Beulah's bed. She raised the storm windows wide open,
that didn't help. Then she ripped off the sheets, threw 'em
right in the garbage. She carried the mattress with the pad still
on it onto the back porch by herself even though both handles
was ripped out. She still smelled it — in fact, she smelled it
the *most*, she said, in the bedboard — had me try to smell it,
too, we was like two dogs smellin'. Tappen, he gone off to
Emery Lane's, said he needed an alternator but we knowed
he just wanted to be with a man, and a man who don't talk.

Doro didn't touch the bedside table, that was sacred ground
to Tappen, even Billy and Debbie knew, no one touched
nothin' there, not even the aspirin bottle, nothin'.

The people, they kept comin'. Shooey Molton passed the
mattress on the porch, and the pad, too, with the dried-up
blood spots, she didn't blink, she come in with a lasagna and
a applesauce. We don't have to return the pan, she was sayin',

she got the disposable kind down at Jamesway in Cartsdale. "Course, you wouldn't throw it out," she says. Nope, course not. I smile. *It's the bull.* I forgot, like I forget Ma or even Daddy, or even myself, how you forget yourself, I forgot him. It's him though, makin' it easier for me, and Beulah, she give him to me, Beulah give him to me.

Doro ain't nowhere when the people come. Billy and Debbie, they're playin' dictator on the porch with the dogs. They yell out orders, the dogs don't do nothin', don't even look. I don't even know some of the people. Laureen, she's takin' the food, and thankin' em, and noddin' polite when they talk on 'bout Beulah.

The bedboard's in the upstairs hall 'gainst the wall. I open the door to Beulah's room real softly, like I'm sneakin' into church. There she is, layin' on the box spring, sound asleep. My Doro, both fists up under her cheek. I lay down with her, careful, I don't wanna wake her up, I curl my knees up 'hind her knees perfect, we was two spoons.

I put my arm over hers. She didn't move a muscle though I knowed she woke up. I didn't say nothin', but it was goin' over and over in my brain, like a chant, like I was tryin' to hold her steady with my brain, over and over it was goin', "Don't you run, I got sump'n gonna make it easier for you, but don't you run."

We laid still a long time, Doro just as still and me holdin' her, she was just as still.

About the Author

Mermer Blakeslee was born in 1957 in the Catskill Mountains of upstate New York, where she lives with her six-year-old son, Hansen. Her jobs have included working as a gardener, a cleaning lady, a short-order cook, a laborer, and a local newspaper reporter. She is employed as a ski instructor and a race coach during the winter months and writes during the rest of the year. She received Columbia University's 1987 Quarto Prize for her short story "Dandelions." *Same Blood* is her first novel.